A DARK STRANGER

JULIEN GRACQ

A DARK STRANGER

Translated from the French by
Christopher Moncrieff

PUSHKIN PRESS
LONDON

Pushkin Press
71-75 Shelton Street,
London WC2H 9JQ

First published in French as
Un Beau Ténébreux
© Editions Corti, 1945

English translation and translator's afterword
© Christopher Moncrieff 2009

First published by Pushkin Press in 2009
This edition published in 2013

ISBN 978 1 908968 35 7

Frontispiece Portrait of Julien Gracq
© Roland Allard / Agence VU

Proudly printed and bound in Great Britain
by TJ International, Padstow, Cornwall
on Munken Premium White 90gsm

www.pushkinpress.com

For Roger Veillé

They that have power to hurt and will do none,
That do not do the thing they most do show,
Who, moving others, are themselves as stone,
Unmoved, cold, and to temptation slow;
They rightly do inherit heaven's graces,
And husband nature's riches from expense;
They are the lords and owners of their faces,
Others but stewards of their excellence ...

Sonnet XCIV
WILLIAM SHAKESPEARE

A DARK STRANGER

During these fleeting, drifting days of late autumn I recall with special fondness the paths on that little beach at the close of the season, suddenly strangely overwhelmed by silence. It's barely alive in its itinerant idleness, that hotel where the influx of women in light dresses and unexpectedly triumphant children will recede with the equinoctial tides and, like September breakers, suddenly reveal the brick and concrete caves, the rocky stalactites, the childish, appealing structures, the over-groomed flower beds that the sea breeze will devastate like dried-up anenomes; everything which, suddenly abandoned to a vacant heart-to-heart with the sea will, for want of reassuring frivolity resume its unassailable and loftier status of a ghost in broad daylight. On the seafront, dead, glassed-in verandas, their wrought ironwork eaten away by the salty scourge, fret themselves like looted jewellers' shops—suddenly, incredibly, the worn out, washed out blue of shutters closed on unseeing windows holds back the ebb of life that's responsible for this decay. Yet in the sourish sunlight of the October morning, sounds spring up, strangely detached from the silence in the same way the solemn movement of a sleeper frees him from a dream—the white gate of a wooden fence creaks, a doorbell echoes loudly from one end of the eager street to the other. I must be dreaming. Who has come calling here with such ceremony? There's no one here. There's no one anymore.

I disappear behind the rows of villas above the amphitheatre of the beach, walk up and down avenues buried beneath the trees on soft brown soil muffled by sand and pine needles. As soon as I turn the corner of the beach an equivocal silence sets in. The rumbling of the

11

sea reaches the depths of these avenues' hollow green pathways only hesitantly, stirring me like the rumble of rioting at the bottom of a sleepy suburban garden. On this background of dark mineral greenery, of pine and cedar, silver birches, poplars suddenly blaze out, reduced to faint golden smoke, spreading their red flames like fiery caterpillars consuming a piece of paper. Soon the great maritime grisaille will restore this whole scene to primary colours—here and there a subtle pigmentation takes hold, puddle by puddle—salt blanches the surface of walls, turns metal railings a jarring red, the sea breeze scatters sand on floors through cracks in the doors—a sudden, unexpected encroachment pervades this little town, harsh and grey like the salt and the coral, with the vague traces of a fire gone cold, of a dried-up tidal wave.

There are colourless afternoons, closed off, sunk beneath hopelessly unchanging skies—like the poor fairy-tale world inside the glass walls of a conservatory—deprived of that changeable layer of skin that the sun creates for them and which prepares them as best it can for life, when the consciousness of the all-powerful reserve of things wells up in me to the point of horror. Just as after the performance is over I sometimes imagine slipping back into an empty theatre at midnight and, in the dark auditorium, catching the scenery refusing to play the game for the first time. Streets emptied for the night, a theatre that reopens, a beach abandoned to the sea for a season weave conspiracies of silence, wood and stone as effective as five thousand years and all the secrets of Egypt for unleashing spells over an open tomb. Hands distracted, holding keys, playing with rings, hands skilled with weights that make tombstones turn, move the bezel which makes you invisible—I became this ghostly stealer of mummies when, as a gentle breeze blew in off the sea and the sound of the rising tide was suddenly more perceptible, the sun finally vanished into the mist on that afternoon of 8th October 19 …

12

GÉRARD'S DIARY

29th June

T HIS MORNING, a walk to Kérantec. Quite deserted
around the pier in the little harbour, the beach that
stretches away to the left totally empty, dunes running beside
it covered in dried rushes. There was heavy weather out to
sea, an overcast grey sky, great leaden waves crashing on the
beach. But between the piers the silence of the swell against
the stone side-walls was incredible; great big tongues, urgent
and rough, yet agile, unsettling, shooting up suddenly like
anteaters' tongues as they reached the sea wall without
warning, exploded in mid-air in an ice-cold spray. I had
lunch in an empty restaurant all on its own in the middle
of the dunes, the raised floor made a hollow sound, the vast
dining room (the local youth must dance there on Sundays)
with its strings of cheerless paper flags, its varnished pine
boards, reminded me less of parties than of a ship's wardroom, the Sailor's Rest, everything which, as so frequently
in this part of the world, (lifeboat sheds for barns, outdoor
pantries built onto every house in the street) brings with it
that unavoidably gloomy, mean, rule-bound character that
so often gives the Breton countryside a mournful look.

As I came back along the path by the shore I ran into
some youngsters from Kérantec walking in pairs, coming

for the dancing. Serious, almost solemn—the girls' hair
flew in the strong wind—hands in pockets; it wasn't
warm. A lonely pathway nonetheless. In the distance,
from the dunes that hang over the track, above the low
line of the roof of Le Retour du Pêcheur you could see
foam flying with the sea's every salvo. An unusual pleasure
spot. Then, among the muffled bombardment of the
waves, in a brief ray of sunshine I heard the tinny sound
of a record playing which—above the uneven bass note
of the tide, in the midst of this great echo chamber of
clouds and water—wasn't in any way offensive. Yet one
girl followed along the seashore all alone in the opposite
direction to the stream of ants. Idle, slow, indifferent,
occasionally bending down to pick up a shell, a piece
of driftwood—or just looking vaguely out to sea, and at
those moments her hands always shifted stupidly to her
hips—what thought was there in that rustic head that was
genuinely her own? In real landscapes just like in paintings I'm
constantly intrigued by the idlers who appear at midday
or twilight, spit in corners, throw stones, hop and skip or
ferret out blackbirds' nests, sometimes darkening a whole
area of the landscape with gestures as unfathomable as
it's possible to be.

After strolling back I had dinner alone—the *in* crowd
had already left for the casino.

After dinner, stretched my legs on the beach for a
moment. A fine beach, melancholy and magnificent, the
windows on the seafront set ablaze by the sunset like an
ocean liner lighting up. The empty sand, still warm, like
a beach of human flesh which you want to walk over,

cover, to soil as artlessly as it does itself. And yet the air is so pure, so purely cold, so clear, as if constantly washed by unseen showers. A gentle gurgling in a furrow in the sand (the tide is going out) tries hard to turn the ground into a flooded landscape—the almost human sound of channelled water cutting into it like a woodsman's axe. I took a deep breath. Ah, what a mouthful! Sand drifted across the dunes, the air snapped like great banners, standing up against the cutting edge of the wind with a feline flick of the tail. And out on the horizon the hurried toing and froing of the waves, always this commotion of foam, this riotous churning, a confusion of clouds lined with squalls and sunshine, this fierce *train* of swells, the unfailing impatience of the sea in the background.

30th June

THE HÔTEL DES VAGUES gets under way, like a ship sailing through summer. There are enough people here now for you to feel the jostle; a makeshift state of mind sets in in this little holiday world. Seen from my window this morning, Jacques tacking off for a swim. Every day there's an early bustling from his room above me—the way you walk into the wardroom unselfconsciously, laugh loudly with that bold upside-down intimacy of bunkmates. But any lack of awkwardness always stops outside Christel's door; no one would dream of knocking on that door until her majestic appearance—the young princess in a towelling bathrobe—gives the *signal*. In every little group of human beings, each vaguely-constituted unit, there's always the one people seek advice from, who they consult with a sideways glance before loosing the hounds.

Christel rules this little world with one heavy eyelid voluptuously closed—so much so that you can't imagine more perfect peace of mind, rejuvenation, than in this precise setting—with its perfectly-formed jaw (the jaw that conveys so well any excess or lack in a person, that jaw so often tactless), perfectly *right*. Once she closes her mouth there's no point wondering whether to expect another word. An extraordinary sense of measure and control. The essence of tranquillity, restfulness.

18

Christel interests me. She interests me because she plays—and enjoys playing. But among the informality of the beach I sometimes catch her eyes shining with *reserve*. What a lovely word! Which suggests to me—and I'd like it to to her—much less the restraint of a good education than the somewhat perverse amusement of watching yourself play your part so well. Rather like, on the level of this mini-theatre, the "Am I a god for them?" of Conti in *Béatrix*—into which Balzac, a born actor, couldn't help but put all his self-satisfaction.

She isn't a goddess for me—but as from tomorrow I intend giving her the chance to prove she's an intelligent person to talk to.

1st July

IT'S A LONG TIME since I opened this diary with such impatience, such a longing to write. I open my window on the night breeze—I've been pacing up and down the room for ages, strong and vigorous, clear-headed like after a bath, alert and bursting with bright ideas, all of them conceited, fleeting. This evening I had a most unusual conversation with Christel.

I already sense how inept I'm going to be at expressing the colour—the nocturnal, moon-like atmosphere in which my memory constantly bathes her. To do so I need to conjure up Poe, that aura of birth and remembering, of a time still obscure, a sequence that can be reversed— an oasis in the desert of time:

> *'Twas night in the lonesome October*
> *Of my most immemorial year …*

… I couldn't start writing straight away. I walked up and down the room again. Out the window the bay is all lit up, a vast arc more than eight kilometres across, it seems as small as a kindergarten paddling pool, the beach shimmers and in the troughs the sea is inky black—now and then a wave breaks with a slip of its oil-black, silent tongue. The arc lights raise a motionless song, upright as a flame, to the planets above, while out to sea the signalling of the lighthouses brings peace to this great expanse of mist and water. The night, calmer than morning, at rest beneath phalanxes of stars.

Christel *is* a princess. At every moment her presence, a gesture, a word, brushes aside any doubt. She's can't move without creating the mirage of a train of respectful obsequiousness in her wake. Even at midnight, alone with a man in the depths of this empty darkness, she's more guarded than in a crowded room. Which removes any unpleasant ambiguity from my story at least.

Did I have any aim taking Christel off on that walk? Lodged in the corner of my being where forebodings and anxieties lurk, all I had was a profound sense that 'it would be interesting'. The day had been heavy, too warm, the deadly drowsiness of a beach senseless with sun—the pinewood was like a cage full of perfume, a vase of smells so strong as to almost make you pass out—like when I was young, going outside on a brilliant June morning where the overly-grand scent suddenly rooted me to the spot, like the road to initiation, the pathway to mystery, the Corpus Christi procession passing our front door. I'd been working, intoxicated, on my study of Rimbaud: I thought I'd identified precisely which obscure maze of rumours, which conspiracy with the worst chorus of earthly fragrances, from which there's no escape, was responsible for some of the poems in his *Illuminations*. This day of omens was very much the prelude I'd dreamt of to a conversation that I only remember as being vaguely steered through long silences, its sudden pauses so difficult to fill.

We must have meant to go as far as the golf course on the far side of the dunes. Vast, gently undulating like the beautiful fleece of a wild animal, almost completely hidden from the sea from which all you can hear is the great noise of the surf on the smooth, empty beach nearby, and whose plumes of spray can sometimes be glimpsed through the thistles amid tremendous thundering. At night it must have been a deserted, empty place. I've always liked walking in the moonlight in such exposed, open spaces.

Christel was wearing a white beach dress, bare feet in sandals. For the first time I noticed a small gold cross on a chain round her neck which she sometimes played with while talking. This little detail struck me, and I don't know why but I could hardly take my eyes off it for the whole of the walk—as if it had a subtle meaning whose significance nonetheless escaped me.

We'd set out towards the end of the evening. The wind had dropped, the air was divinely cool. Heading north—the direction of our walk—you soon leave the houses behind. It's almost rural there—low houses with vegetable gardens, farmyards, garden tools, sometimes a cock crowing in the daytime. Then immediately comes bare heath, a desolate landscape, almost dramatic, all the more naked for being traversed by a line of telegraph poles.

The conversation got off to a bad start. First the members of the 'in' crowd filed past without the slightest sign of benevolence from Christel. She talked to me about Jacques.

"Undoubtedly the most remarkable young man here. And yet he's still a child. I feel at ease with him, like someone from school."

I poked gentle fun at Jacques. Jacques is the hotel poet. His room is apparently full of esoteric books—and the corridors either reverberate with lavish offerings of *jazz-hot* or the most outrageous contemporary beats. But after talking to him a few times I came to the conclusion that he does it deliberately. To be frank the boy hasn't read a thing.

"What does it matter? Jacques is only interested in difficult poetry. Of course for him it's not a question of making sense of it, but I think he's trying quite rightly to reach a certain depth. That's all I try to do too … "

A pause, then: "I don't know why it is I like certain things. Other than that's the way they present themselves to me. And it's always something you can take or leave."

Christel is quick to turn a conversation into a monologue. I admire the easy way she seizes the dice. She belongs to that breed that can't be interrupted. Besides, when she wants to she talks with real seductiveness.

We crossed the dunes, very stirring in the moonlight, their great undulations so dignified as on the day after a battle. Grey mist hovered on the distant horizon as on the far side of a clearing in a great forest massif.

"Who'd think of going for a walk in this part of the world on a night like this? What I've always loved most in the best-known landscapes is the place that's sometimes the most difficult to find—how would you put it?—where you *turn your back* on the view? In Venice, in that maze of little alleyways that are so strangely muddled up with the canals, for me it was the lovely moment where the alley turned into a passageway, where you walk past doors in that suspect, slightly seedy intimacy of a hotel corridor—a cheap hotel with a jug of hot water, a slop pail—and at the end, through a dark, arched doorway, the whole of Venice is as one in a little square of black water, shimmering and twirling in the sunlight with a tireless lapping sound. It's the same here, there's nothing I like more than those long clipped lawns beyond the dunes where you turn away from the sea—so stately, so stilted, but with the great sound of the sea nearby, an endless backdrop. And in those little channels of black water where the tide comes in without a sound."

"Were you in Venice for long?"

"Yes, Venice was my early childhood in a way. We used to go back there with my mother nearly every autumn. For as long as I can remember my father has always had the curious knack for coming and going. Always weighed down with business, directors' meetings—a ridiculous life of sleeping cars, luxury hotels—a fashionable beach for a few days occasionally."

"I'd like to hear about your childhood, Christel." (I'm writing this as a kind of commentary, leaving out the parts where I wasn't keeping the conversation going. What's the point? I've always thought that most of the time dialogue is a virtually unguided monologue—in the grip of their demons one of the two always wields the sceptre, as they say in the best literary salons).

"I've got very few memories of my early childhood. But when I was twelve I do remember being in this big, depressing boarding school—long, starkly-lit corridors, chilly courtyards overshadowed by lime trees. It was a dismal time. I had very little idea how to make friends— and my week, every week (and I was a good pupil mind you) was spent waiting for Sunday morning, visiting time. After mass we'd play in the courtyard. The janitor appeared with a list of names, and it was the chosen few. I hardly ever went out, I lived in a state of permanent uncertainty. The minutes went by, the janitor's appearances got fewer and fewer as the courtyard got emptier, taking on an atmosphere of impending execution. And that was that. I remember that courtyard in the rain, enclosed, disenchanting, cut off from the world. The most isolated, emptiest corner of a wood wasn't as isolated, as empty as that feeling of abandonment. And so I'd walk under the dripping lime trees. I can still remember their glistening trunks even now, running with water, dark and hostile, soaking wet twigs lying on the ground, bark peeling off, unending torrents pouring from the branches. I was drunk on loneliness, on stifled tears. I used to watch the clouds go by in gusts of wind, sometimes a stronger gust would shake the branches, spray the sodden ground with great big raindrops. Outside were busy streets, the enchanted labyrinth of the town, cafés, theatres, the crowd, beautiful places where life takes shape, gets tangled up, leans on other lives, takes their shocks, their warmth—it was everywhere I wasn't. And yet I knew how disillusioned I was each time I went out, as if a curse followed me through the streets, a mark of banality and disinterest. Yet there was always this obsession with a thousand possibilities, a free, charmed life protected by a magic spell inside those high, merciless walls whose harsh shutterless windows all glimmered.

"Then the teacher on duty took us back to the classroom, a crippled little flock, shorn, shivery sheep, the symbol of abandonment. And how despite herself her voice got lower, more familiar, from not needing to carry so far (there were so few of us left), for me it was like a forlorn caress. I used to mutter to myself: 'Poor, poor Christel!' At that moment I felt myself becoming totally devoted, good, helpful—for a few minutes the terrible injustice flung in the face of my childhood turned me into a sister of charity.

"I was thirteen when I was taken to the theatre for the first time. I'll be brave enough to admit that my taste, among the (apparently) least excusable operas, leads me instinctively, boldly, to the worst, the ones that don't *compromise*. They were doing *Tosca* (it makes you think doesn't it—but I forbid you to laugh). As I came into the auditorium I walked straight into real life, the only one I want to have. I love everything about the theatre: the strong perfumes, the rush of red plush, the half-light of a shiny, pearly cavern, cut off, laminated like the inside of a seashell or a beehive. Wherever I find myself in a theatre, the maze of corridors, the sloping floors, the staircases all make me think I've come in through an underground passage, and that's vital for the sense of security, of perfect isolation I get in there. That church scenery in a theatre that's already a church, for me it crowned the profane music with a kind of religious aura: it touched every fibre of my being at once, it was Sacred Love and Profane Love (be good enough to believe I'm not joking) like in certain naive paintings—I'd have liked to burst into tears but I stayed rigid, dry eyes wide open, as if an electric current was passing through me constantly. I'm sure there's part of the score (but to my shame I don't know where) which seems as if it ought to belong to some innocent entertainment, like a village fête on a bright sunny day—yet at the same time I felt myself plunged into a Rome of heat and smells, of vast, pitiless high walls (I've since seen Piranesi's *Views* and the Castel Sant'Angelo, but that night I imagined them) beneath a lethally stormy sky and luxurious passions— so I don't know why that particular part, why that little island laughing in unawareness, balanced on the heights of a disaster suddenly seemed grimmer than the most tragic lines, so much so it made me shudder. The last act shattered me. It was life in death, life after death, a triumphant hymn to love even *beyond* the coup de grâce. I'm not ashamed to admit that when the conspirators are uncovered by the extravagant theatrical gesture at the abyss into which the heroine has just thrown herself, it was this stroke of genius in the worst possible taste that finally reduced me to tears. I was there at the heart of the tragedy, beyond life, totally carried away. It was a matinee performance in winter: when we got outside it was dark, my mind was buzzing, I kept bumping idiotically into walls like a drunk. The city and its lights reeled under an avalanche of blackness, in the suffocating cracks in its glimmering red avenues, to the triumphal flapping sound of a flag at half mast."

I looked down my nose rather at Christel, although I was touched by such a passionate, contemptuous confession. There's a warm, gentle mockery based on strictest complicity, one you don't have to admit to—which just comes from the need to dispel any excessive sympathy.

For a while we sat in a hollow in the dunes. The sand was incredibly white, already cold like a snowfall in the glorious moonlight. The tide was going out, you could hardly hear the sea. The haziness of the landscape, lost between the open sea and the misty horizon of moors covered in pearly dust, was beyond compare. Christel was lost in dreams—borne away by some sad thought. She spoke in snatches, with long intervals of silence.

"Maybe I'm wrong to say this—giving voice to your thoughts is rather like making a vow—but I think I'm destined to wreck my life. I'm far too unconcerned about things that don't matter. It's as if I'm throwing nothingness back into nothingness in a sort of rage. 'Lost time should be lost. What's empty should never be turned to profit'. That's my kind of nobility. What wouldn't I give to be able to float, sleeping, above the boredom of life, all those moments when you can't help thinking you could be somewhere else."

I pointed out to Christel that her haughty disdain could just be laziness and a lack of courage. It's only by keeping life at a high level of tension that by way of reward we reach those special moments, the chance of a miracle, those dramatic events that I could tell she'd been thinking about for the last few minutes.

"And what makes you think this 'tension' is so low in me," she replied, mockingly, smiling at the unseemly turn the conversation was taking. But she'd already moved back behind cloud, taking on that nocturnal, hushed voice, so resonant and unruffled that I can't describe it in words.

"I don't really believe we make our own luck. It passes us by too wonderfully. I'm a Calvinist on that score (she smiled as she spoke, a strange fixed smile). I'll tell you another story. It's a moral tale, although its value lies in getting the details exactly right. One night I was coming back from Angers to Nantes on the fast train. About halfway there's a part of the landscape I love, where the Loire narrows between some large wooded hills with chateaux at the top, a very royal valley. I was on my own in the corridor looking out at the dreary rain-streaked night. As so often I was 'talking to my inner self'. I live alone and often do that. In conversation I can never think of an answer till it's too late, so I come up with my best oratorical gambits that way, and sometimes I get oddly worked up. I imagined I had someone to talk to, and began preparing them for an effect of the light over the Loire which I've often noticed at this spot. 'Oh what a shame, it's such a shame the night's so dark'. And precisely at that moment, precisely—in the space of two or three seconds it became as *clear as day*, an apocalyptic light, a disturbing magnesium light all the way to the horizon. I stood there white as a statue, not moving my arms or legs, as white as you'd be at the sound of the last trumpet. There's something so terribly forceful about improbability that I think you can be sure I'm not making it up. The next day I saw in the paper that a meteor had passed over the Loire and apparently came down in the sea about a hundred kilometres away. For the rest of my life I'll never forget that supernatural 'that's no problem'. I rank the meteor along with my sign of the zodiac."

We came back along the dunes. Her long, elastic stride, so stately, so haughty, made me feel elated. Having no idea what time it was, certainly very late, I kept thinking I could see dawn breaking. Christel teased me gently for falling under the meteor's spell. Her clear laugh burst out in the night, we trod down the long grass between the large bare patches of the dunes, white as salt. And it's true I'd have liked to keep on walking till morning.

3rd July

THE DINING ROOM at the Hôtel des Vagues is unusual, with its wood panelling, the décor of *a day in the life* of a ship's cabin, and at the same time with that grandeur a room acquires from having a large staircase incongruously in the middle. I like it particularly on these rainy summer days, in the light from frosted windows, where a huddled, bored intimacy finds its way through the skimpy beach clothes, the atmosphere of an evening in the country, a mountain refuge hut in a sudden snowstorm. Lunches drawn out by shivery cold are conducive to camaraderie.

Which is how I ended up smoking at Irène and Henri Maurevert's table. Young marrieds. Him, tall, quite elegant, somewhat lethargic, somewhat vague. Although I have to say not without attractiveness. I've had some quite long conversations with him about Rimbaud (interesting to note how successfully this man of letters—I'll explain my use of the expression if you like—has played the part of a man for all seasons in our time, a 'forum for inquirers and the inquisitive', that he'd have laughed at if someone had predicted it). Perhaps, beneath an over-attentiveness that in other ways is so kind, touching, he's already rather bored with Irène. It's the little things, those little things that are everything: the drumming of fingers on the tablecloth when the long-awaited coffee threatens to prolong the tête-à-tête too much—the occasionally over-indulgent glance out to sea from the picture windows—the first, as yet-discreet appearance on the table of keys, paperwork, private correspondence, business correspondence, newspaper cuttings by which a honeymoon couple heads into that state of duplicity with which, as forty approaches and caught unawares through a half-open door, a well-off middle class family wrestling with their private after-dinner outpourings is more or less fraught. Yet Irène is physical, lively, seems to tackle each new day with carnivorous good grace. It's obvious she'll always be unaware of any kind of altercation with life. With her, whatever the topic of conversation, after a few minutes Henri takes on the expression of a man pushed into a corner. I love catching fault lines between people at their source: nothing more irresistible than the desire to drive in a wedge and then, inevitably, with a few blows of the sledgehammer … Irène! A strong woman, and I dare suggest a sensuous one.

It wasn't long before the conversation turned to Christel. My mind still full of our encounter the night before, I probably did my utmost to steer it in that direction. Henri seemed to have little interest in the conversation, but as soon as we started talking about Christel I detected a glint in Irène's eye. I'd swear she knew about our little jaunt the other night—she scoffed in veiled terms at the interest I take in that 'young person'. She'd apparently known Christel well at boarding school, had stayed 'on good terms' with her, which I think is part and parcel of those polite friendships that whither and turn to disappointment once you pass eighteen, and which are the chosen territory for the worst female treachery. Perhaps driven by a liking for complicating the game, for introducing pointless motivations purely out of love of the art, something you see so often in women, she tried to pique my curiosity about Jacques. "Christel is very much to his taste, you know. They're forever swimming, playing tennis together. Everyone thinks they'd make a lovely couple. All the same I don't think Christel could make a man happy. She's a woman who lives from one impulse to the next. Literally. A cerebral type. To my mind there's nothing that withers a woman more quickly. Nothing that burns a woman out more quickly than contempt. And Christel is contemptuous; she's a princess, distant, a Sphinx. But I wouldn't want to put you off, my dear Gérard."

Her friendly concern enchanted me. So was I mistaken? In this hostility I detected something more than the usual rivalry between women. Impossible to see Irène, this magnificent brunette, without immediately being aware that she's above all *the woman*, with all the appetites, the needs, the blinkered vision of her sex. Not even the most banal, hackneyed gallantries could fail to spring automatically from the lips of someone faced with a woman who's been more mercilessly *depersonalized* by her sex than anyone I've ever seen. I don't wish to be improper—yet it's perfectly obvious that that mouth, that backside, those breasts rebel against the thought of appealing to anything except the brief caress of a palm,

33

lips, words of sexual arousal. And what makes most women proud, Irène experiences as humiliation. Tucked up so snugly in her prison of flesh, she's got something against Christel for being able to play the angel, stir the imagination, dreams, more directly than the senses. It's a sign of a far and away rarer jealousy, because prejudices scoff at it, which I think I found in that word "Sphinx" which she used with such scorn.

One day I'm going to write a moral tale to suit modern tastes: *Beauty and the Beast*. A story of female jealousies where they claw each other to death as in the time of the Bacchants. It'll show the tribulations of a saintly soul struggling vainly to escape her prison of seductiveness—having a fit of humiliation because she senses she's gradually going to *become* what she appears to be, and tearing her rival apart, who's swathed in ingénue impoverishment, the somewhat scanty charms of the Platonic Ideal. Epigraph: *'Dramatis personae'*. You've got to laugh. But I'm being unkind to Iréne. Her perfume smelt exquisite—the kind I prefer on her: violent. If only we could accept ourselves as we are, make intelligent use of what nature has given us. There's no other kind of genius.

As we got up from the table Gregory, with that falsely indifferent manner of his, that fugitive look worse than any pleading, came over and suggested to Henri and I that we have a game of miniature golf. I've noticed how much this biblical prophet, this haunter of ghosts, likes silent games. Pipe between his teeth, overjoyed and contemplative—a mass of composure and visible

34

reserve—I can imagine him turning over a single thought indefinitely, one that punctuates this lethargic game without interrupting it. He must think the way you chew. Solitary, awkward, a pulse that you imagine being slower than other people's. Yet through being engrossed in his musings, settling himself on his legs, sucking luxuriantly on his pipe, he ended up beating us by several lengths. With a slightly red-faced formality that found it difficult not to burst out into triumph he offered us both cigars. Dear Gregory! I think he's delightful.

4th July

I GOT UP EARLY to watch the sun come up over the bay. For me the main attraction of this hotel, set back from the seafront whose dull roar is never out of earshot, is its beautiful garden, the lime trees, the cedars, the simple flower beds. Above the expanse of greenery a corner of pink roof was so wonderfully rural in the light of dawn that I wanted to applaud. The whole morning was glistening after a shower of rain—between the reflections of the trees the asphalt of the drive took on an immeasurably soft shade of steel blue. Everywhere cockerels introduced the paths of the deluxe beach to the passing courtesies of mid-morning; you got the impression here and there, from the boulangéries with their little dog carts, whistling waiters setting out chairs on café terraces, gates of villas clinking, of a kind of affable Montparnasse mixed with early-morning village humour.

I met up with Jacques near the beach huts. With lots of laughter, lots of splashing we pounded into the cold baptismal water together like young dogs, and then headed back to the rickety huts with plenty of back-slapping. Then, coated in sand, side by side in the morning chill, we solemnly smoked the first cigarette, like passing round the peace pipe, delighted with each other's company like two young pages who've just jousted together in a hearty rough and tumble of muscles, that soothing horseplay, aware that the best part of the day is already behind them.

I sensed that like me he wanted to talk about Christel, that he was groping around awkwardly to broach a subject that wasn't close to his heart in any remotely normal way. But of course the taboo was the most exciting thing about it, and after a few unsuccessful attempts he simply plunged in head first.

"What do you think of Christel?"

Reckless!

"I don't think anyone here is in a better position than you to have an opinion on that."

"Don't I know it. She's my holiday romance, right? That's what everyone here thinks. It's odd. As if Christel was someone you could have that sort of relationship with. You might as well try (he was choosing his words self-consciously), try and take a red hot iron from the fire with your bare hands … "

I started. From what this comparison, this clumsy confession suddenly revealed of the scandalous, I straightway gauged just how far Jacques's mind was from the good friendship that everybody assumed existed between him and Christel.

"Christel's disconcerting. I can't think of a better word. She's young yet sure of herself. Her gestures, her face, the sound of her voice have a lot to do with it. How can I explain the strange impression that captivates me? Of course older men sometimes give you the same impression, but what's surprising is the power of suggestion, the supremacy in one so young. Don't you agree?"

37

"Not only do I agree, I can't imagine a clearer way of putting it. But it wouldn't overly surprise you if at the same time you suspected there was something else in her."

He lit a cigarette.

"Shall we go for a little walk?"

"Let's."

"So you're interested in Christel too. Don't deny it," he went on, effusively, "I know it, I'm sure of it. And it's got nothing to do with jealousy."

He smiled.

"I don't think that's quite your style, or mine."

And then from my lips came those astonishing words that I still feel I wasn't quite responsible for—

"She's not made for you or me ... "

We stopped. Jacques looked at me oddly. The landscape faded in the dull shadow of a passing cloud. The empty beach was suddenly cold, dismal. What a strange turn our little chat had taken within just a few minutes, for no apparent reason. I got the distinct impression of one of those unexpected detours in a dream where you walk gaily through an open door—and all of a sudden, on the other side, stretching out of sight is an extraordinary icy landscape, a land of plague and nightmares in a poor, mournful light.

"Why do you say that?"

I don't know why instinct prompted me not to tell Jacques about my night-time conversation with Christel. *He doesn't need to know.* I felt myself becoming a young boy again, one who wants to keep his very first secret at all costs, like a treasure.

"I don't know. You're aware I hardly know her. She seems a very secretive young woman. I don't know why but I imagine she's following a path that could take her heaven knows where, but neither you nor I have the power to stop her. When I say you, I probably owe you an apology—after all I could be wrong. You've probably met people—and they can be as friendly, sociable, hospitable as you like, but at the first glance, the first word, you thought: 'We've nothing in common, there's nothing possible between them and me'. We've often talked about literature, and I think you remember the meeting between Romeo and Juliet—

> *What lady is that which doth enrich*
> *the hand*
> *Of yonder knight? …*

"It's the classic example isn't it, the exceptional example of love at first sight. But there's *always* love at first sight. Although I think that in a way that's not necessarily tragic, which is often very far from tragic, the first glance that two people give each other, a certain intonation that creeps into their voices, quite insidiously, as fatally as a poet's inspiration, binds them forever, for better or for worse—or perhaps for total indifference. The sports pages sometimes talk about an 'indian sign' when two athletes meet for the first time, which creates a permanent, secret pecking order between them, a fascination with inevitable failure, a sudden failing of hope. 'What's the point?' The outcome is already decided—that's how it is—that's how it'll always be. This person will be a plaything for me—for

39

that one I'll be king, to this chance acquaintance I'll have to give an account of my actions like the steward to his master, and even the most confident of my actions will seem hollow if it doesn't get his seal of approval, a certain glance that puts my mind at rest. This one is a powerful person but I'll never talk about him again without a note of contempt that would cut him to the quick if he heard me. According to my secret code this despot is actually a fool, that skivvy a prince. This one is invisible—I'll always look through him as if he were glass—he speaks but he's far, far away—as he comes closer I dismiss him from my world with a frown."

"And there's no appeal against this sentence?"

"There's never any appeal. No one dreams of making one. How can the inexpressible express itself? Besides, it would make them die of shame, humility doesn't sink that low. Everybody knows an Aunt Sally when they see one and everybody respects them and, what's remarkable, feels in some obscure way ennobled by them. Everyone litters his path with gods and corpses, no one comes back from the dead, and even the Bible claims that archangels still keep their inviolable crown when they fall."

I'd got quite worked up, and pretty stupidly at that—whatever got into me? Jacques doesn't like me. He went off pretty coolly. He'd have forgiven me for saying something unfair—but how can he forgive me for pitying him without good cause? No one takes kindly to being told: *you're as bad as the rest.* I must be a complete fool.

5th July

S PENT THE WHOLE MORNING brooding over my fit of prophesying yesterday. Jacques must have had a good laugh at my expense afterwards. But he didn't say anything at the time. He was 'impressed'. A nice hot bath, a lively game of tennis (Jacques is now fighting hard to get the better of Gregory) probably drove any odd notions from his mind. And yet?

Could this mean I won't get away with it so lightly? Today I felt extraordinarily depressed, all alone in this idle little town where I don't know anyone and which I've no use for, where I've ended up for want of anything better. I was intending to get down to work on my study of Rimbaud, but literature bores me. And it's more serious than that: I'm getting old, it seems as if I've slipped imperceptibly from the time you spend living into the one you spend watching life go by. Of course, there are still lots of things that interest, fascinate me—yet it seems I'm already gently letting go, that I'm no longer totally in the running. I find myself working out how many hours have been wasted, lost in a day, my capital utterly squandered. Dismal thoughts for which there's no cure. Yes, I'm well aware there's 'the meteor'. But it's when you don't yet need to believe yourself that you deny the value of time so fearlessly.

Time, it dragged all afternoon. Towards evening I went for a walk past the lighthouse at La Torche. Once beyond the lighthouse all signs of life suddenly disappear, and a great arc of beach bordered by dunes stretches away, an entirely bare landscape, oppressively empty, shaking with the thunder of great rolling waves on the idle sand. Beneath the grey sky, between ocean waves and waves of sand it was like a beach road threatened by the sea, the magic circle of an atoll, a snapshot taken in yellow light while crossing the Red Sea. Here among this isolation, this grandeur beneath heavy, runaway clouds, you couldn't help but imagine ... I don't know—the smoke from Shelley's funeral pyre behind a fold in the sand, or Gauguin's stately line of bareback riders, their long-legged, noble movements astride the sea's equine brothers, dappled and brusque as her waves, those great horses that in ancient legends come out of the sea in time of disaster.

I lay on the sand, let the dulling disaster of the waves wash over me. It's enough to occupy you completely in itself—first comes the anxious wait for them to break, for the steaming torrent (*Ah! It'll be even better than the last one!*) Jumping for sudden wild joy, that stomach-churning joy brought on by anything that comes crashing down (the childish pleasure I felt during the war—the sole innocent pleasure—on blowing up a bridge). Then comes the savage, biting, pitiless sucking-up of sand by the salty tongue—the sound of the earth being washed, thrashed, redeemed from lethargy, from anything that isn't absolute purity of honest, upright rock, until it's grovelling, until this blonde with bone shoes is as prostrate as a figure on a tomb. Images of an equally childish desire, so fundamental: a liking for bare bones, scrubbed skulls, washed out like a bowl till it can be filled up, drunk from, a liking for burnished skeletons with a beautiful patina like old pieces of junk, a liking for delving beneath disappointing flesh until the hammer strikes home—the gentle sound of a pick swung vigorously into turf—me as a child, chewing at a fruit stone till I felt sick.

Yes ... all that ... What's the point of fine words? I'm bored and I'm going to leave. Who's keeping me here? No one ... so—so it's best if I leave before it's too late. In the end there's nothing but triviality all round me, although this place, the pallid beach, the hazy moorland, the silence of the avenues shrouded in leaves has something sinister about it. I sometimes get the impression I'm in a waking dream.

The day after tomorrow I'll pack my bags.

How the clouds weigh down on the earth this evening! As if a canopy of unmoving vapour has gradually sunk to the ground. Chill, overcast summer days without a breath of wind—for some reason I see the days of my childhood, nearly always lazy Sunday afternoons—the garden, its cool darkness, its unmoving greenery; a gentle glimmer over the motionless River Loire, the fluffy trees and fields of June. Walking along the paths of our lovely garden in my Sunday best I used to wait for the sound of the bell for Vespers—past a bend in the Loire you could see a steeple, so slim against the skyline, and in the north you heard the sound of a train. That's all, and my heart is about to break. What's happening to me?

43

6th July

A S I WALKED OUT of the dining room Gregory came up to me:

"They say you're going. You're leaving us in the lurch so soon?"

"That's right. I haven't fixed a date yet. I've been called back to Paris—and believe you me I'm sorry to have to end my holiday at such short notice."

"Shame. We'll all miss you. The young people … (Gregory winked in an attempt at cynicism whose utter failure delighted me.) The golf … But since that's the way it is, could you tell me when your room will be free? Forgive me for being so rude—but this is the reason for it."

And he handed me this strange note:

My dear Gregory

I think, I hope this letter will take you by surprise in the depths of your customary idleness. So shake it off and do me one last favour. I've got to spend a few weeks by the sea. Believe me, I'm putting some formality into words that seem grand enough in themselves. With a woman, and I know the ridiculous smile that will greet these words of mine. Sadly, with what distaste! … But let's be clear, Gregory, 'it's not all over for me yet'. I'm telling you that again now, firmly, seriously. You'll see. All it takes … a cool calm head, a steady pulse. Don't tell me I'm feverish again. At first I imagined a wild coastline, a remote house; it was important—the sea, the clouds … you know the kind of thing—but there'd be things to worry about, practical considerations that I've decided to completely dispense with. Make a note of that. So book me a room at this vague hotel, at the Hôtel des Vagues (ah! I like the name I tell you). I assume it's comfortable—ridiculous to ask, but anyway! I'll leave it to you to arrange for us not to be disturbed at all. I couldn't bear that. I intend us to be like oysters in a shell or nothing! The silence of the grave. Otherwise I'll smash the furniture and … but we'll see. I've got other things to worry about. Anyway, I'll tell you everything, but … stay calm. We've still got time. Now off you go, the rest is silence (remember that). Yours

Allan

"Well!" I couldn't help saying as I handed the letter back to Gregory, astonished. "Your friend's quite volatile."

"You don't know him. Ah! It's … look I'm sorry but I absolutely have to find a room for him. I know him, he'll never forgive me as long as he lives." (I didn't get the slightest impression that Gregory was joking.) "It would call our whole friendship into question."

"But he's a maniac, a plate-smasher. What's all this frenzy for?"

"Allan's like that. You don't know how right you are when you say frenzy. Although … in a way there's nobody more well balanced than him. But he's a man, just a man! … Forgive me," (Gregory gave a lovely smile, elated, demure, intriguing, which I'd never seen before) "the very idea of annoying him is unthinkable to me. You'll see the kind of person he is … "

"As it happens I will, my dear Gregory, because I'm very much afraid I'll still be here the day after tomorrow. So don't count on my room."

Another stroke of my perverse genius. Although I'd definitely decided to leave. But suddenly I felt an almost vital need to punish his infuriating smile, that look of being in seventh heaven. So there you have it!

What an odd smile! Perhaps it was that as well; I was filled with sudden, inexplicable curiosity.

7th July

A SUDDEN DESIRE to gamble drove me to the casino this afternoon. I like the brand new, unpretentious white building, I like it for the silence of the surroundings, the birdless pinewood that stands in front of and around it—I'm not averse to isolation, a slightly bleak setting for a pleasure spot. Deserted coral beaches, the solitude of a dark forest—the heart-stopping isolation of a railway station on the taiga, these are images that come to me continually the moment I give in to the dangerous power of the saxophone or muted trumpet that the local jazz—the pride of the casino at G—is so full of.

While the couples dance to the lush sound of brass that so easily makes you swoon, I like letting my gaze wander over the tips of the pines, across the wide clearings in the trees to the reddish-coloured moorland that surrounds this little town, this narrow strip of pleasure, so closely. I've always regarded the pine as a tragic tree. The harsh, violent twists of its branches, the stiff foliage, those tiny sword knots in place of leaves which are reproduced so miraculously in Chinese engravings, not the slightest concession to the softness of flora, a style more in keeping with hard stony ground, gunflint, a scorched existence, something charred, like the embodiment of some primitive notion of love: barren, exhausting, relentless—

47

But love to me is a pallet stuffed with pins.

At high tide at five o'clock I was virtually alone on the empty terrace looking onto the bustle of the beach. The band was playing *Stormy Weather* and suddenly I felt incredibly melancholy. The taste of a town in Asia, tumbling into the sea amid a clutter of junks, like a harbour with its froth of corks and driftwood lapping in the tide in the evening sun, its labyrinth of roofs, masts, rickety verandas, powerful scents in which all life's struggles are resolved—its dark perfumes. Perfume: one of the few things that for me *enriches* life. Our civilisation's incredible timidity when confronted with smells. A perfume by a great couturier: you can measure by that alone how much modern sensuality has withered. It takes the whole weight of the Catholic tradition to continue to impose a fragrance as corporeal, with such assertive presence as incense without causing a public outcry.

At the baccarat table to my great surprise met Jacques, who with an assumed casual manner—well well—was playing for high stakes. What it is with this boy? Is he Christel's (impressionable) holiday romance, a modern poetry aficionado, the best tennis player in G or a fashionable young delinquent? Or is he simply the Adolescent, following the well-known rules by being deliberately complex?

When I got back to the Hôtel des Vagues I admired a magnificent shiny silver car parked in front of the steps in the courtyard. Oh yes, that's right! Gregory's guest. The wild man. But at least a wild man with good taste.

This evening I enjoyed going to lengths over my appearance. The Hôtel des Vagues is a fairly formal place, in the English style, where you dress for dinner. Although it's also still very *vieille France* with its highly respectable cellar and a provincial bonhomie in the way the flowerbeds are laid out, the delightful bric-à-brac in the corridors. I was even lucky enough to be given a lovely Bas-Breton room with box bed pannelling, alcoves, long fabric hangings and a canopied four-poster (pretty incredible I agree, I can see why Gregory tried to get hold of it). Whenever I go in there, room service being meticulous, it's always the half-light of summer in the country: outside the closed shutters you imagine wisteria, the roof of a shed red with Virginia creeper, an avenue of lime trees from a Turgenev novel—then I open them and there's the blinding light of the beach, a Sahara of salt and striped fabric in the bracing snap of a sandstorm, the hubbub of a caravan setting off. I like my room.

There's nothing like taking trouble over washing and dressing to put you in a good mood. I tucked into dinner with a healthy appetite, engrossed in a magazine that nonetheless dealt pretty unceremoniously with my latest book. Then all of a sudden I was vaguely aware of a *strange* silence in the room. Of course, such silences aren't unusual among regular guests in a hotel, particularly if a women comes in and especially if she's sporting a new dress. But in this long silence there was suddenly that indefinable element which distinguishes a pause in the conversation from the horrified lull before panic breaks

49

out in a theatre. Or for someone with a bad heart, that skip in the heartbeat which lasts a tenth of a second too long and thrusts them against the wall, face drained, wild eyes filled with that meaningful look, '*Will* it happen again?'. I'm not exaggerating. I looked up, came up for air. Accompanied by Gregory, two new guests walked in. Him, the image of both strength and ease at once: my first thought was that he walked with genius. The only other person I've seen honour the ground with such harmony was a Slav athlete walking into the stadium during a cup final at Colombes (breathtaken, the entire stadium went "ah!") She—it's too little to say—she's very beautiful—beautiful as a dream. The second thing that occurred to me, in a sort of panic, was that what I saw in front of me was something more complicated, more astonishing than the harmony of the planets: a couple, a royal couple even. The third was … no it wasn't a thought, it was a bubbling, a fizzing in the blood, those blurred eyes, lifeless hands and dry throat you get when the great tragic actress, the Olympic champion appears decked magnificently in their symbolic attributes, and when you just say to yourself—and the whole crowd stiffens, holds up their heads at the thought alone: "There she is, it's *her*—there he is, it's *him*".

15th July

EARLY THIS MORNING I found myself wandering around near the kitchens. I like such appealing places, reminded perhaps of certain, almost crystal clear memories of childhood: the jingling of silver cutlery being gathered up in the depths of a hot drowsy afternoon in that mournful inertia that sets in once friendly guests have left. On my way back to the hall I bumped into Gregory and Allan going out. With that long, lithe tread of his, distant, inaccessible, I imagine him leaving some kind of slipstream that would be unbecoming to cross. They were both very quiet. They headed for the beach. Why did I feel myself *pale* slightly as I saw him? I leant at the window of my room nearly all morning: before me was the entire arc of beach and, among thousands of people all the way along the sands I didn't miss a single footstep on that unfurrowed backdrop. It was the same once at Ouessant, the island with no trees, where a long way off from my hotel I suddenly saw a woman in a black coif come out of her house at the far end of the island and quietly close the door. And on this veiny network of well-trodden paths, so clear, so peaceful under the sky, you can trace the patient progress of tiny black figures from minute to minute like ants in the nest, like those little flags you stick into maritime charts every day to plot the course of vessels on the main shipping lanes. And I actually believe I found myself looking for Allan in that anonymous crowd. No, not him! He *couldn't* be a black dot in the crowd, conform to this muddle even for a moment. Surely, I thought, he'll suddenly come raging through this anthill in a furious swirl—that terror-struck fracas just above the surface in lakes, those little crests of water as a great man-eater heads out to sea.

For several days I haven't been able to get the idea of life in decay out of my mind. It's probably this beach, not quite moored to the sun, this ill-defined strip of habitation, this sucking insect from the backwaters which drains a body of blood as soon as the hot weather arrives. Like you see on posters in railway stations in July, all along the coast of a tiny, human-scale France, swimmers with their backs to the mainland, gaze drawn mindlessly to some swirl of mist out to sea (caption—'*Beaches of France*'), that strange continental tide that coincides with some new conjunction of stars— and then the cotton wool atmosphere of fine, overcast days—my nocturnal conversation with Christel. Yes, but for the last week all that has taken on a particular *tone*.

Don't worry, Gregory, I'm not going to leave now. Allan and I have something to say to each other. It didn't take me long to guess who it was that arrived on a cloud—the one who relieves me of my torments for a moment, of any concerns about not being *elsewhere*—the one who'll put everything back together again here—the one whose face I only had to see to know it represents a *violent* view of life. What can I not expect of him now, the one who persuades without speaking, keeps me occupied without being there? I'm not the sort who judges people by their actions. What I need is more and less: a glance that makes the whole world reel, a hand that stills the sea, a voice that wakes underground caves? What secrets, standing out to sea like spectres in the midst of a silent whirlwind, bind you to the one you brought here, and which enchant her? What shores did you leave behind for his sake, the one whose *presence* is going to be a miracle for me? And you, lovelier than the day, that irrevocable and everlasting beauty wavering as if on a cliff top— what light has he lit inside you that you should cast these giant shadows, spaces at the mercy of your appearances and disappearances day and night, that you should turn my life into a patchwork of light and dark, of wind on my cheek, damp darkness, like a man travelling alone through enormous forests?

No, I don't want to be anywhere but here now, to breath any air but this, the air of a forest after an evening shower, this exciting, icy air that I've been drinking for several days like you breathe in after a bath.

I'm well aware that Christel is as susceptible as I am to the charm of this strange couple; or at least to Allan's. Last night for instance, as conversation turned to them as we left the casino her indifferent silence was revealing. Her few brief words, almost severe, also gave me the impression that she regretted her confidences the other night—and I think I realized that this regret was most of all for having less to give to another person from now on. Does she love him? I only mean does she love him *already*, with that irresistible desire to give, to gather everything together, to throw all of yourself by the armful at the feet of the one you love, the desire that suddenly makes even former gifts seem miserly.

Within a few days Allan has become the idol of the 'in' crowd. At the Hôtel des Vagues that's what they call the group of sporty young people, great dancers, great swimmers, great tennis players who up till now acknowledged Jacques as their leader. Note that a certain *difference*, an openness to a sphere completely alien to someone who rallies other people, a certain aptitude for stepping over obstacles, easily marks you out as the leader of any kind of closed group, a clique. Hence a certain liking for obscure poetry quite naturally made Jacques the first mate, forbade anyone from questioning his choice of jazz records, his views on fashionable ties. But how can he get the better of Allan? The moment he appeared at the casino, on the beach, he reigned by tacit approval as legendary as his style. Every day they wait, hope he'll favour them with an appearance. He gambles, swims, dances with a kind of intoxication, an uncontrollable anger, yet always shut off within himself, alone in the midst of a vortex that's closing in. This morning I watched him on the diving board. I love the moment when a man presents himself to the sea, upright, streamlined, with sudden haughty solemnity, a mustering of his strength, his humanity in the face of the elements, then leans forward like a plank rocking before he springs. Yes, I watched Allan at that moment, his eyes half-closed in an exquisite dream, face secretly joyful—and I sensed the water was calling him—and this fall, this dissolving in which the vertical water penetrated him with sensual pleasure so intense that he couldn't help but close his eyes in a movement that was pure animal, full of grace. The ability to express desires in such a direct, stirring way is given to very few people, in my view as a great and rare privilege; and for me, therein lies the whole fascination that's exerted, particularly but not exclusively over women, by certain individuals who in some obscure way are more in tune with the leap of the animal, the sway of the branch, with the lizard who escapes the water for the safety of the rocks—and whose alarmingly agile body is like creeper that still clings to intertwined, primeval branches.

16th July

MET JACQUES WHEN I went for an early swim this morning; the beach was still empty, we were alone. Impossible not to remember our strange conversation about Christel—and that inescapable memory, which both of us were determined not to mention, now made us awkward. Our own *importance* has declined so much since then—and from our joint fall from grace blossomed a cluster of thorns that would make the scrub in the Australian outback green with envy. We avoided embarrassment by leaping into the water, lightened our mood with a frantic race in which I managed to beat Jacques by a length.

Gentle exhaustion in my shoulders, a great limp exhaustion in all my other muscles, smoothed by trickles of water. Sleep! Sink. During the war, in those terrible wartime cattle trucks that were a living hell of planks, sharp edges, of jolts, the great, all-consuming dream was to lie down in the water like in a meadow, an underwater meadow. '*To sleep in the sea*', as Eluard says. '*To sleep in death?*' During the war there were times when there didn't seem to be much difference.

Sleep. My first night as a prisoner—my one and only memory of great oceanic sleep. It was a damp meadow, a great sea of grass, a meadow full of asphodels on a fertile night in June. We lay in a circle like peaceable cattle,

56

divinely empty minds given over to thoughts of the world, the coming solstice, the seasons. Divine indifference: the sun will rise tomorrow—so sleep! Little island of men, with its guard's sharp upright sword in the great stillness of night, the earth rejoicing in the depths of this peaceful kraal—and yet it was a georgic hymn which rose from there, rolled up, shrouded, comforted in a mantle of grass as far as the eye could see, suddenly more like the gentle cooing of a storm than the sound of gunfire.

Looking out my window this afternoon, elbows on the sill, for the first time I was aware of the extraordinary theatricality of the beach. The narrow strip of houses with their backs to the land, this perfect arc formed up round the great waves where you can't help wondering how the sea could possibly be more resonant—the alternating hubbub of the tide swarming over the beach one moment and leaving it empty the next. Then there's its particular perspective: as in a theatre it's arranged so you can see everything from every spot. Terraces of a Coliseum laid out for watching some staged naval battle. Suddenly I find something bizarre and thrilling about this trivial comment. In this perfect curve I'm looking for a geometric centre point, that flaming hub where the radii of this semicircle converge—and what else? The liturgical gestures of a celebrant, the priestly calling that a simple killer of bulls in the ring can't help but assume when with the slow steps of the sacrificer he comes to the centre of this vast oval to be set ablaze, and which a single flame where life is rendered down to its highest point of tension purifies, freeing ten thousand hearts at once.

Leaning out I saw Christel just below me, also with her elbows on her balcony, staring at the beach. I'm sure, absolutely certain, that it was *him* she was looking for—him, always one of those thousands of black dots, temptation and perpetual torture for eyes in which everything comes down to the fundamental question on this basin of dry sand—and which slip dizzyingly along the rim of this merciless racetrack bend—this great patch of Sahara that throws up handfuls of salt and scorching sun.

This evening I spent a few hours discussing literature with Henri Maurevert. After a few half-joking, half-serious and in the end rather uncomfortable allusions to "our unusual guests", he started being quite offensive about women. In a very general way of course, and with the best intentions. I've noticed a nonchalance, an indecisiveness about him which has been getting more marked for some time: the off-putting way he has of leaving long silences in a conversation and only picking it up again half-heartedly—like a cigarette butt you try unenthusiastically to get one last drag from—is pretty rude. Beneath his highly elegant exterior, that lunar element he has about him, erratic, crumpled, struck me particularly tonight. The impression I'd formed of him as a bored man has changed most peculiarly and precisely to that of someone *out of his orbit*. Made for moving in the wake of a domineering woman he seems to hover on the cusp of a new star's sphere of attraction—on the edge of one of those *in-between states* that are the only kind of abyss that satellite personalities understand.

18th July

I N RECENT CONVERSATIONS with Gregory I've probably shown too much interest in Allan. I felt all the less obliged to be reticent about him because of the efforts I've made to not mention Dolorés (thanks all the same, Gregory, for being the first to tell me her name). I've sought out Gregory's company a lot these last few days; his childhood friendship with Allan is one more thread that links me to The Couple, prevents me from straying into the desert—as long as he and I keep talking to each other I feel slightly less insignificant. Can't help thinking: if Allan and Dolorés were to meet *us* now it would be impossible for them to do otherwise than come up to us, say hello to *us*, hold out their chests slightly under the subtle goad of that little ruse called vanity, see how low this 'up-and-coming young academic' has sunk. All it took was a kind of high-flying *metic*, maybe a pair of ritzy thrill-seekers (for the last few days I've been becoming bitter. Dolorés left yesterday—for a few days, maybe a few weeks Gregory told me. Ah! May the heavens …)

I've pestered Gregory so much that this morning I got a fairly long letter in which the fine young fellow apologized for having to go away for a few days and, knowing how interested I was in his friend, "took the liberty" of offering me a few pages on which, the night before, he had taken it into his head to jot down "a few memories, a few thoughts and a few predictions—if that's not too strong a word". Standing holding those pages I blushed slightly for a second, like a child caught being deceitful—very much *red-handed*. Could I credit Gregory with such shrewdness? But curiosity about this windfall soon got the better of me.

I'm reproducing his fascinating piece of detective work more or less as it stands. Because, quite unintentionally, that's exactly how Gregory's memories of his friend seemed to turn out. To testify at which trial—to help in which mysterious inquest? I couldn't shake off the slightly sinister impression it made on me, this dubious, so sudden and inadvertent shedding of light on a suspect. It's always those closest to us who betray us.

Allan Patrick Murchisson was born in Paris in 19.. of an English father, recently naturalized, and a French mother. His father managed theatres and seems to have been extremely wealthy. Allan's childhood was undoubtedly spent among incredible luxury, that lightweight, fickle, slightly unreal luxury that adapts itself to constant moves, a life of travel, expensive hotels, fashionable spas, friendships with actors, writers, virtuosos as passing as they're dazzling—the atmosphere of the court of the young fairy-tale prince whose lack of any real substance can't have been immediately apparent to Allan. He was such a lovely little boy, fêted, pampered—he adapts to life so wonderfully—he has that cheerful animal quality, the grace of a young creature let loose who can be forgiven anything and which he still finds in himself today when he wants to, when he recovers a certain (yet how very well-controlled) spontaneity that makes him so irresistible to women.

But for the sake of accuracy I prefer to stick to what I know about him, what I saw with my own eyes. There are so many myths going round about him.

I first met Allan at school. I can see him arriving as if it were yesterday. We were all dumbfounded by his style, his blasé manner, his violent, savage, unrestrained thrusts at life, at every kind of pleasure. Whereas we, inside the high walls of this bleak prison which, believe me, it wasn't easy to escape from for even a few hours, we'd resigned ourselves to staying buried in the depths of this stagnant pond for several years—for him that gaol of ours was never anything but an open place whose gates he could mysteriously unlock whenever the fancy took him. For him the most sacred rules were waived. He went out whenever he wanted—perhaps his father had some hidden influence over the Father Superior—perhaps, and that's what I tend to believe, he even cast a spell on the guardians of the all-powerful rules. For him life never stopped penetrating, flowing through the walls of that school, like those young prophets blessed with miraculous visions which we read about in the Bible. Even on weekdays (you appreciate how outlandish that would seem to a boarder in a well-run private establishment), the gates would open for him through the workings of some special act of grace—for a play, a concert, a society gathering that it was indispensable for him to go to. Surprising thing—not one of us abandoned boys held it against him. On the contrary he was the gap in the bars of our cage, our glimpse of sky—to follow him through those divinely-blessed streets, unknown, touched by a light we couldn't imagine, those forbidden treasures, that fairy-tale kingdom that the Town represented for us outside the disillusioned hours of our monthly day out—I actually believe we dreamed more dreams, had more wonderful adventures, that in the presence of this graceful freedom we didn't sigh about being chained up. He was our permission to dream, to hope and to try, our lungful of outside air, our permanent ambassador to Wonderland.

Allan was a brilliant pupil, but his place in class, the prizes, the awards left him oddly indifferent. He'd created a specific culture for himself—beginning by immersing himself in the most obscure, most arcane, most daring works of contemporary literature while he was still young. At the time I knew him this Rimbaud who fascinates you so much held few secrets for him anymore. So from the start his childhood excitements were marked out by something that was in an odd way clear-sighted. *Perhaps he never* dreamed *with the opaqueness of true sleep, that childish belief, the mystery that settled over our ink-stained desks. Later on he gave me to understand that for as far back as he could remember—and this revelation had a particularly painful effect on me—he'd put his dreams* to good use. *The classic authors on the other hand, who were the glory and torment of the school, left him totally unmoved—perhaps he never read them. He read with rapture, quite carried away—I can see him now, wide-eyed, that intriguing swirl of books on his desk, that randomly-selected orgy, an appetite for anything and everything from which he emerged to stride round the yard with us in a kind of deep, hazy exhilaration, a mist shot through with vague flashes of light.*

Somehow—I was a devout child, quiet, devoted to my lessons, with an instinctive sense of proportion—I think it soon occurred to me, in that state of excited restlessness with which we felt him moving, *living among us—that Allan was 'burning life at both* ends'. *During his conversations with me—such serious, brotherly conversations in the school yard, one arm round my shoulders, the memory of which can suddenly reduce a grown man to pulling the most appallingly pointless faces—he would often come back to the peculiar idea, almost an obsession and so unlike those of someone his age, that you could use up your life. In the drama of childhood, a drama whose final catastrophe is simply life itself, disillusioned everyday life, he already clearly foresaw the final act—just as later as a man he would sense above all the approach of its final event: death. (I think I ought to apologize here for such rhetoric; but you've already realized that Allan is no ordinary person. With someone like him you can't go back over the slightest memories, the vaguest trail without suddenly coming up against unexpected, mysterious exits—like a mythical forest suddenly solemnizes the merest footpath with shadows, allowing the sun to shine down its shaded paths as no more than a shimmer, some kind of strange mist from off the high seas.)*

In a young person to whom life was going to grant so much, this was undoubtedly the origin of his remarkable restraint. Now is the moment for an anecdote that I find significant. Allan's good looks were no advantage to him among the ferocious school population—or perhaps they just attracted that secret, chaste devotion between children of the same sex which is aroused by certain striking physical attributes and which for me has always been more mysterious and cruelly unjust than love—but as I said, he often went out and it was no doubt during one of his unforbidden little sorties into the town that he met a young girl, almost a child. There's nothing to make me think they even spoke, but she knew he was a boarder at the school, and every day she walked past the high, grim walls in the disused lane overshadowed by the school gardens. A quite poor girl, but with an appealing, innocent face, and who I'd sometimes noticed through the railings on top of the wall. Allan looked out for her every day from a particular overhanging branch of a lime tree, where I can still see him, crouched like a young jaguar. She would look up and their eyes would meet—but in Allan's eyes there was such a dangerously equivocal glint, so affectionate and yet so cruel, that the poor child daren't stop and walked on, blushing furiously. I'm pretty sure this scene of primitive fascination was repeated over several weeks— then the game, if that's what it was, stopped because of some chance event—one of those sudden transformations *that aren't uncommon in childhood—maybe she was ill, or Allan's mind was suddenly elsewhere. For me the extraordinary thing about the episode was that I was the only one in on the secret— again chance had something to do with it—and that Allan never dreamt of taking any vain pleasure from it, which at that age could have been particularly intense. And believe me it wasn't because he was incapable of bringing the escapade to a halt.*

As endearing as Allan's personality was—he made devoted, disinterested friendships that would last a lifetime—from time to time a sombre, savage side to him would appear, a kind of grave humour that he managed to carry off frighteningly well, and which the following little story might illustrate for you. With us as with most other schools like ours, it was customary for the big boys *to rag the new ones—perfectly harmless most of the time, since adolescents have an innate sense of how far to go which tends to get overlooked, and which life subsequently goes out of its way to warp—in which a spirit of inventiveness, imagination, and more often profound character traits emerge in quite genuine inventions, perhaps the only* masterpieces *that that awkward age can produce. The dormitories were divided into small cubicles by wooden partitions that only reached halfway to the ceiling—a curtain on a rod closed off these very basic* loose boxes *from the central aisle. At night there was no monitor on duty—respect for other people's sleep was left to natural discipline. Among the new arrivals that year was a quiet little boy, very shy, very awkward, one of those sickly boys, oversensitive, with a delicate girlish face, as helpless as a blind man as soon as they leave the maternal environment. From the moment he walked into the school yard, where he bumped into the walls like a bee on a window pane, bewildered by the empty spaces, by that hard, Sahara-like crust of a school playground, the big classrooms full of empty desks, the dark smell of ink, the ringing flagstones in the cloisters where he was frightened of making a noise with his clogs, I noticed Allan watching him with an alarming look in his eye. That night, helped by some other boys he got an enormous glass demijohn from the kitchen courtyard which must have held the school's supply of cooking oil for a whole month and hauled it very carefully, empty, into the* new boy's *cubicle. Once the demijohn was set up, enthroned on the unmade bed, it was carefully filled with water. Full, it weighed a good sixty kilos. Once it got dark in the dormitory, already full of steady breathing, we settled ourselves in the next-door cubicle, hearts racing, and clambered up the partition to keep an eye on the recipient's bed. We assumed he wouldn't be able to bring himself to go to bed, to* undress, *blushing like a Christian virgin stripped naked in the arena, for his first night alone—the night of terror—until it was completely dark. In the shadows the demijohn took on a spectral appearance, huge, black—an incredible fungus growing on the white sheet, so sure of itself, so well-established, so final, so shockingly* present—*that you'd have to have never been a child to not understand how we trembled with expectation, wild delight, panic and* fear *at the sight of our handiwork. Eventually the dormitory door opened very gently, pushed by a faltering hand, and hesitant footsteps crept awkwardly, so slowly towards the cubicle. Gradually, timidly, we heard our victim pull the curtain—then, turning round—he* saw. *I'm sure he stood stock-still for over two minutes, arms dangling by his sides, motionless as a horrified statue, listening to the terror-struck pounding of his heart. The breath froze on our lips. A tiger hunt couldn't have created anything like this electric atmosphere, our eyes out on organ stops. A moment later, after what seemed like an eternity, we saw tears running down his face in the darkness, silent and hurrying, like a fountain. And then silence again, stillness. Eventually, walking like a ghost, he took a step forward and, closing his eyes like someone throwing himself into an abyss, he* touched. *We heard his fingernails chink on the surface like a glass against the teeth of someone with fever—then shoot back as if from an electric shock, and we knew he'd now plumbed the depths of terror. Another lengthy pause during which he must have felt his flesh weaken, dissolve, then, like in the antique legends, and no doubt after having spoken, like Ulysses, like Hippolytus, to his deepest heart, he* went to the monster, *and with his ridiculous little arms like an avenging* Hydra, *he shook it. The demijohn rocked unconcernedly on its round base and, drop by drop, taking its time, began to spill ice-cold water on the sheets. Waking the savage horde whose snores surrounded him was out of the question. And so, his child's heart pierced by more hurt, more helplessness, more distress by this discovery of human treachery than by the awful phantoms of the night—with a pathetic,* well-considered *gesture of utter desperation, silently he folded his little arms. And from the top of his perch, like a cockcrow, we heard Allan's wild laugh.*

But he no doubt quickly became aware of the power he had to push ideas and things to their worst limit without any effort on his part, that power to unsettle *life—and I think it was in reaction to this dangerous tendency of his, which at times I noticed he couldn't control, that he instigated a curious form of Anglomania among us—which the island ancestry he was so proud of was able to justify, and which established him as our prince of style once and for all. He cultivated impassiveness, an elaborate* cant *adapted for schoolboy use, wearing a monocle, Eton bow ties and suits with an English cut, a kind of hard, chilly elegance whose extraordinary refinement he probably knew better than anyone how to bring out. A strange state of terror took hold in the class when, surrounded by his staff of snobbish young delinquents he decided to turn what, body and soul, had long been his* dominion *into a vulgar British India. At a stroke a whole caste of untouchables were removed from his sight and, cast out from the sun, languished in permanent Coventry—and while exceptionally a few 'natives' enjoyed the privilege of being treated as juniors, a small phalanx of 'Whites' massed in closed ranks at the back of the class, crop—the badge of their authority—in hand, devoted themselves whenever necessary and from behind a mask of impassivity to keeping the hoi polloi[1] in line with a well-aimed blow to the legs. From time to time Allan would glance at this scene from the last days of the Roman Empire with the half-closed eyes of a bored archangel. After which, having establishing this incredible dictatorship, he abdicated.*

Towards the end of his time at the school I found him more and more secretive, remote, so much so that the slightest contact with

*a classmate made him scowl with disgust. He never discussed his
thoughts with anyone, always brushing aside any serious topic
with a frosty look, but I remember that the thought of death, and
especially the funereal pomp that goes with it, seemed to have
an odd fascination for him. One day someone fell awkwardly
from the trapeze during gym, fractured his skull and died a few
hours later. Since the family couldn't be told in time we decided
to take turns keeping vigil over our friend for the first night. Allan
naturally took the first watch—but the next morning, not having
thought to wake anyone, he was still there at dawn, eyes fixed on
the dead boy's face, nostrils puffy from the heavy, cloying smells
that rose from the wreaths, lost in some obscure state of rapture.
He got a stiff telling-off—but stuck to silly excuses, the most
convincing being, because there was a certain naive truth in it, that
he had 'lost track of time'. Yet I always knew that this diligent,
all-night childhood confrontation with oblivion, which left him
pale and changed for days afterwards, must have been a milestone
in his life. Much later he talked to me about the 'unforgettable
moment' when dawn crept into the chapel and the expressionless
face among the wreathes and swathes of flowers 'came back to
life', 'as if time had been reversed'. But what he meant by that,
what conclusions he drew from such vivid impressions, no one will
ever know.*

*I don't know what became of him after we parted outside the
school gates—I don't want to know. He became a diplomat, had
a long and brilliant career, an enviable position. But for some time
he'd had a reputation with women for such unrestrained, brutally
shocking immorality that here I'd prefer to just give an account of
that part of his life when I saw the rough outline of the man he
became having the finishing touches put to it. What truth there may*

be in these disturbing, ugly rumours I couldn't possibly know—
I'm in no hurry to know. For me it's enough to believe that Allan
could only really be guilty on another, no doubt infinitely more
serious, more appealing *level, of those* misdemeanours *whose*
youthful extremes I've tried to describe to you, and which for a long
time he seemed to constantly swing between, undoubtedly always
ready to bring all his strength to bear on the first point to give way
under his attack, yet also supreme master of himself, reserved,
calculating, one of the most constantly unpredictable, the most
receptive *people I've ever met.*

As far back as I can remember I can't shake off the feeling
that Allan is someone who's marked out *(but for what purpose,*
what task?), one of those individuals who are made to goad
the most level-headed people into a kind of mysterious, twitchy
fortune-telling, a prophetic trance—something to which these
pages probably seem to you to sadly bear witness. The direction
his life has taken is without doubt not the same as other men's.
If you fold a piece of paper in half you get a straight line; but
if you fold it again and again the straight lines eventually create
a spider's web in every direction, a star whose rays all link up at
the same central point. I've lost hope of working out where that
point is, but I've never stopped believing that however deeply he
might seem to be involved *in life, Allan is capable of holding on*
to that ubiquitous quality, the casual plenitude that can make his
path cross mine at any moment—which makes it possible for him
to catch up with me here.

Since I'm in the mood for metaphors, I'll use this one. One day
in rhetoric class our teacher dwelt for some time on a comparison,
which he probably regarded with a certain self-satisfaction, between
the inferno *in Dante's* Divine Comedy *and the idea that the*

Romantics, particularly Hugo, subsequently had of it. To him the essential difference seemed to be this: whereas Dante imagined the circles *of his inferno getting continually smaller as they spiralled downwards, like inside the bowl of an anthill, to the final well where* Satan wept with six eyes—*Hugo, in an unusual inversion of this image, makes the spirals constantly* get bigger *as they make their way to the depths, unleashing the imagination in a maelstrom, a fit of vertigo, a gigantic hazy disintegration into darkness. From the insistent way he stressed this practical detail I couldn't help thinking that he saw it, rather curiously, as the touchstone of the modern mind. And however clumsy, unexpected, out of place this metaphor might seem, Allan's life, what I can make out about it from his jealously-guarded thoughts, the ultimate consequences which, against my better judgement, I look for in a life that I could only have had the vaguest clues about for a long time, certain gestures, certain unnerving attitudes, invariably send me and my imagination chasing reluctantly after this spiral.*

At this point I want to put an end to the outpourings of an imagination that you probably find over-excitable. I still have a confession to make. I'm not just going away for a few days, like I said yesterday. On second thoughts I don't think I'll be coming back. You know how much I was looking forward to seeing Allan. But as I've found him so much altered, so odd, so hot-headed (his letter had already aroused my suspicions), on the verge of an event, a decision that's already occupying him and whose extremely serious nature I can only guess at—for the moment I'd prefer us to go our separate ways. I don't know what will happen once I've gone. I don't see any good coming from this sudden, purposeless visit, like a bird fetched up on the coast by a storm out to sea. This sudden pause *in the middle of an existence that's*

71

always so hectic—this suddenly loose, relaxed hold on life, when he knows so well how to blindly plunge his claws into it—and then the drowsy disinterest he shows in conversations I've had with him, the look of a sleepwalker in broad daylight—and lastly there's that woman, so exceptionally, so extravagantly beautiful. He didn't want to tell me a thing about her. All this is shadow and maybe it's silly to be frightened, yet I admit I'm leaving because I'm afraid. And I think I'm justified, in confessing this to you who I know to be so sceptical, so calm, essentially so level-headed, in trying one last conspiracy; by somehow entrusting this person to your care, a person so captivating, so unstable, and perhaps also so unprotected against obscure dangers.

So here I am, entrusted with a soul! I read the letter again, carefully, but can't find enough justification for its sinister conclusions. And yet this tone, this certainty? Has Gregory told me everything? I somehow get the feeling that his remarks, which at first sight seem so disjointed, are dictated by some all-consuming idea which Gregory has his reasons for not revealing. Reading it, it's as if, strangely, a meticulous painter obsessed with detail has painted his own portrait in front of a mirror and then inexplicably insisted on blanking out the figure. All that remains is a reflection on a stage set, the impression that a shadow is moving around, invisible yet at ease, among a collection of incomprehensible objects where everything gives it away.

19th July

YESTERDAY I FINALLY got acquainted with Allan.
It had been cold and misty all afternoon, and
at a table by myself in the smoking room I was trying
unenthusiastically to solve a chess problem—a three-
move according to the Indian strategy I assumed, a
particularly tricky Holzhausen. The key kept eluding me
and I'd got to that peculiar state of irritation well known
to chess-problem solvers: something in my dignity made
me inclined to *declare* the problem unsolvable.

Allan came in behind me without a making a sound—
I think I vaguely saw him sit down and flick through a
magazine—then suddenly I noticed him leaning over
my shoulder, peering at my algebraic scribblings with
extraordinary perceptiveness. The question obviously
interested him.

"Would you think it sacrilege if I contributed something?"

"Please do."

He's certainly a first-rate problem solver. He soon found
the crucial square, and the mechanisms appeared in this
basic governing fact, which is stunning for one thing and
seems to illustrate better than anything how much of
a *revolution* discovery is. I suggested having a game. He
plays outstandingly, preferring closed games, the Sicilian,

the West Indian, like all players who sense those secret relationships between squares which lie dormant on the chessboard, that latent explosive force that sleeps inside every piece, the instinctive understanding of which gives the game of wunderkinds like Alekhin, Breyer, Botwinnik all its superiority over chessboard *mathematicians* such as a Morphy or a Rubinstein. Maybe he also wanted to delay the outcome out of pure good manners, and thus chose to make an unspectacular start. Nonetheless I still lost fairly quickly.

We ordered drinks and chatted. As always when I play against a strong opponent I tried to get him to reveal the secret of his game. To which he replied quite rightly that since the greatest maxims of chess are never more than a comment on a master's game, an *a posteriori* reorganizing of genius, they can't ultimately be anything other than what a solution is to a problem. This one from Niemzovitch for example, perhaps the most profound and widely held—and probably applicable to most other things as well as chess: "Never reinforce the weak points—always reinforce the strong points."

"Do I take it from that that you think it's possible to make the transition from a game that's so insular, protected by such arbitrary, even bizarre rules, to everyday experience?"

"In a certain analogous way, yes. I think you can *feel* the world as if it's the square of hieroglyphics in a chess problem where a secret mechanism is buried, dissolved in external appearances—where the discovery of a particular focus totally changes what you think about the power of the pieces, the perspective of the squares, like the turn of a kaleidoscope. You only need to put a piece on a random square for everything to change. From a certain point of view that's absolute magic. What's more, the workings of a mind that struggles to create such a closed world for the sole purpose of surrendering its *effectiveness* with the wave of a magic wand is something enormously revealing. It's a world suspended, outward appearances blurred, whose very *existence*, its framework, if you look at it closely, depends only on the revelation that's waiting for it to come along."

"I'm with you completely. But aren't you exaggerating the significance of something that might just be a liking for the difficult, the subtle, the secret? You know those games children play where a shape is hidden in the branches of a tree, the cracks in a rock, and you try and find out what it is. It's stretching things a bit far to see that as the sort of pentacle you seem to have in mind."

"What I'm talking about is actually quite different. The game you mention remains totally external to the pattern that exists before it—this, in contrast, tries to free itself from it as if from an adulteration, from a body that's foreign to its substance, to cut itself off from it, expel it. What I have in mind—and it's not just a question of a problem—is this unavoidable impulse to search for a *perfect*, invisible work, the golden key that you only have to touch for *everything* to suddenly change. It's been quite clear to me for a long time that in every work of art, a book for example, there's such a key. There's matter for serious reflection in the fact that a masterpiece is recognizable—among other things, more

75

than any other thing—by certain proportions, or rather unusual *disproportions*, to my mind absolutely irreducible to external art and, incidentally, quite rudimentary to the composition. When I'm looking through a favourite book I sometimes get the feeling the author is leaning over my shoulder, like in those games we used to play as children, giving me a wink to point out where I'm 'taking short cuts' or wandering off the point. I'm convinced that if I could *see* this phrase in its true light, perhaps the central, focal word that always eludes me and yet which, running through the weave of the style, points out certain grand, concentric circles to me like a kite hovering above a vast expanse of countryside—then I'd be able to sense them *changing*, these pages whose hidden secret moves me deeply, and begin the voyage of discovery from which there's no return. Maybe new magnetic forces would disrupt the hesitant constellations of print that showered the pages, ultimately depending on a series of coincidences whose utter randomness we can't possibly fail to see—who knows, perhaps the *completion* of a work, like in Poe's *The Oval Portrait*, brings about a person's death? Who can tell what conjuring power is concealed in the watermark of the text, that magnetic, invisible text which guides the poet unconsciously through the chiaroscuro of the written word, already so full of dangers. Every work of art is a palimpsest—and if the work succeeds, the text that has been erased is always a magic text.

"Now I'll draw your attention to the fact that for probably as far back as we can go, there have never been dreams without a belief in a *key to dreams*. People's opinions only began to differ over what this key might be for. A dream also has this fundamental peculiarity—which it's impossible not to describe as 'significant'—those unforeseen angles that wound and alert the mind. And if in the end this key just opens the gates to a mundane earthly paradise—love, money, travel—it's probably only because, as in the case of the ordinary reader, people treat as formulas that apply to the world here *below* something that obviously only assumes its true significance on a *higher* plane.

"There are plenty of people" (here Allan's voice became even more neutral, colourless—and in any case for a while it had been hard for me to work out whether he was still serious or just joking—but I found remarkable charm in what he said. To be more precise, I thought with bitter irony that I sensed he was trying to cling to these fantasies like a drowning man who feels himself sinking to the bottom), "people who weren't mad, who believed they could claim the world was a dream or, which amounts to the same thing, that the world was dreaming. Yes, for a long time I've had an idea at the back of my mind that there comes a point in it where everything is revealed, some lever that gives you a hold over it. You could imagine searching physically for life's points of attachment, the world's nerve centres, a sort of telluric acupuncture. That was the belief for whole centuries—and those are perhaps the only ones where I feel it would be a delight to live. The earth retained its mystery but the mystery *could* be overcome, like you overcome a woman in a sense altogether different from the metaphorical. There *was* an earthly paradise, but not made from the soft stuff of dreams, not from the hollow flesh of symbols—but with the green leaves of real trees, the refreshing delight of real water, and *settled*, like in the hollow of an armpit, the flexing of a groin, in an inexpressible fold in the virgin earth. The mystery of the world was hidden inside itself, but no longer symbolically, hidden the same way as the sex is in a woman; and like a lover guided by the physical certainty of his desire the unstated aim of the great explorers, Jason, da Gama, Columbus, was perhaps nothing more than the drunken, solitary *possession* of the world.

"I'm someone for whom myth has no meaning. I can't imagine how people feed on this incredible deception— how that need for revelation which plagues humanity could be satisfied unless it *sees*, unless it *touches*. You can't satisfy your hunger on places where the hero of a legend *once lived*. Thomas actually touched Jesus's wounds and, it's ridiculous to say, Christianity would never have taken shape on this earth if Christ hadn't been incarnated. For there to be Christianity there had to be Christ, born in *this* village on *this* date, who showed *these* pierced hands to the doubter and vanished from the tomb in a way altogether different from the metaphorical. How could he have been convincing without his inimitable *presence*? The quest for the Grail was an earthly adventure. The chalice existed, the blood flowed, and at the sight of it the knights felt hungry and thirsty. All of this could be seen. With which eyes apart from these physical eyes could I ever understand a marvel? The marvel, the great marvel for me is that people can serve themselves up this diet of dubious characters, such appallingly colourless spectres that the mind plays tricks with—this century's mind-spirit of renunciation, truly the humblest there's ever been, the one that turns divinity into a character from its own mind. I can't be satisfied unless the two halves of me are joined together and—since you like Rimbaud—unless I possess the truth in a soul and a body."

The cool, offhand tone in which his astounding monologue came to an end left me bewildered. In the most perfectly natural way Allan lit a cigarette, and with a half-bored expression began putting the pieces back on the board.

"It can't have escaped you, my dear chap, that all this seems to call for a conclusion. Of course that couldn't take any other form than an act. You'll see," he added in the most extraordinary tone of voice, getting up. "How beautiful the sea is this afternoon." And, forehead resting on the window he sunk into a silent reverie. For him I'd clearly ceased to exist.

20th July

I GOT UP IN A BAD MOOD. Eyes half-open I saw the dull grey light of a wet summer morning, one of those empty holiday mornings that always seem to make insomnia worse. I think I dreamt about Allan: is this person who's preoccupied me for the last week going to force his way into my dreams as well?

I didn't like his manner yesterday; not one little bit. There was something offensive and absurd in his breezy self-disclosures. He was quite obviously talking to himself in front of me, he wouldn't worry about such a *minor thing*.

And yet I'm sure there wasn't a single phrase that he hadn't weighed up, scrutinized. He was trying to create an effect—he hopes to gain something from this odd behaviour he puts on. He wants to arouse people's curiosity, make use of the ambiguity, the riddle of his presence here.

A strange memory comes back to me, of a friend who went into the priesthood. The day he made the final decision he dragged me off on a long walk round Paris. We talked about modern art and, usually so reticent, his eloquence knew no bounds, he talked powerfully, fluently—and the more he said the more I sensed he was making it up. Like a criminal instinctively concocts an alibi he was hastily *transposing* his feverish excitement, but it was the fever itself, this elation, which gave him away.

What could he have in mind if he thinks he can *do whatever he likes?*

I'm now more or less certain he's talked to Christel. For quite a while I've been planning a trip to Kérantec with her—we ought to go and see the little harbour and have lunch at Le Retour du Pêcheur, so strangely remote in the middle of the dunes. But Christel has been avoiding me, like she's been avoiding 'the crowd'. She's shut herself away in her room for whole afternoons, becoming distant, unapproachable—preoccupied out of all proportion. This morning she finally decided. I realized she suddenly needed to talk—while I needed to get my mind off Dolorés, off this incurable anxiety. What's become of her? I needed to talk to a woman about her, needed that gentle assurance confirmed, repeated by another person, that she'd really, actually *come*—that her abrupt disappearance was more than just a worthless trick with mirrors, the whim of a ghost.

We walked along the top of the dunes. It was a pleasantly warm morning, hazy, drowsy, the sea sparkled beneath banks of mist. The harbour appeared—a clutter of unpretentious whitewashed houses scattered randomly on the heath, completely bare, not a tree, not a bush—just wrapped in gentle trails of mist. It was Sunday morning—and all along the road Breton sailors were playing boules behind the cafés, careful and silent on this dismal day off. Dressed in blue, salmon pink, a little group hanging round by the pier, nothing to do, hands in pockets, were looking out to sea. And I thought that if it hadn't been for their sense of what was right and proper keeping them on dry land on a day of rest, they'd have liked to slip into their boats and make off out to sea, drift, get back to their everyday gestures out on that smooth, empty ocean—so awkward, so tied in knots did they feel on this ramshackle earth with its miserable pleasures. But Sunday in Brittany isn't made for going to sea. The streets echo with the dull clatter of clogs—and we both felt as much at home as two lost souls are ever able to in this world.

Nothing more wretched than the streets of this gloomy port. The hard stone where clogs ring out, hard, low white houses where a door half opens and you get a glimpse of a pine partition separating two miserable rooms. Then the street quickly disappears into a vague moorland track, where nets still flutter in the wind; and you hear the loud flap of washing dancing in the breeze. This is one of the world's real outposts, where cloth and hides go mouldy in the damp air, the drab, idle yawn of a fort in the Sahara.

We stayed silent. It began to drizzle. Hidden by mist our path even had a tragic look about it.

Le Retour du Pêcheur was empty. Nobody in the vast dining room with its varnished pine partitions. From the long picture windows all you could see was leaden sea and a narrow strip of close-cropped coastline. No more than a skeleton, bare bones, the basics, utterly stripped—just the constant gliding of the clouds, cropped grass quivering and a sea *'that always changes'*. I reminded Christel of the beautiful line from Flaubert's *Salammbô*:

The Celts missed the three rude stones beneath a rainy sky at the end of a gulf full of islets.

This great empty room, echoing, half-asleep, which intimidated us so much that we instinctively took refuge in a corner—where every voice seemed to echo too loudly—the great low clouds pierced by the glimmer of an uncertain sun that hid itself away, the yawning, sleepy waiters, the suddenly dismaying impression of being adrift in the rain, disoriented, out of season … we'd definitely *washed up* here. Like a wedding guest who, in the evening when the jolly mood brought on by all the singing, laughter, the memories evaporates, drags himself off to a table for one in a restaurant, heart bursting with nostalgia. This is where you turn your back on life, feel yourself gradually dissolve into the cotton-wool mist, the fine, relentless, never-ending rain.

What had we come here for? We sensed we had nothing to say to one another today—each left to our downward path, making a sealed chamber for ourselves out of these blurred, muffled spaces. Mournful gusts of wind shook the windows. The afternoon drew on, yawning, ageless, sky blue. You could hear the magnificent rustling of the great rolling waves, a sound like poplars in a high wind.

We talked about our travels. Christel told me which countries, which cities she'd like to see: Constantinople, a place she'd fallen in love with before even getting there. As I looked at her I could see her gradually roughing it out, planning, already *leaving* on this journey that she'd decided would be her next holiday—she was really passionate about it. Suddenly I felt bitterness coming on.

"Forgive me, but wasn't Allan Murchison at the embassy in Constantinople?"

She blushed quite openly, suddenly flustered, emotional—then tried to put on a brave face, tears welling in her eyes.

"Yes. He's quite an extraordinary man isn't he?"

"Quite extraordinary."

But I thought it would be unkind to take the subject any further.

22nd July

I RÈNE, WITH THE GENTLE TOUCH—the gentle touch of the naive go-between—it had to be your idea, as if it were the most natural thing in the world. If something can be done then you should get on and do it, shouldn't you. Faced with the Valkyrie's ring of fire, you're the type who'd think it's simply a matter of hitching up your skirt and making a jump for it. And it's true. You *can* always jump.

I was lying on the beach after a swim, reading a novel, busily roasting myself, when I saw Irène coming towards me, clearly quite excited, lips bursting from holding back a smile.

"Shake yourself, you lazy good-for-nothing. We're going to the Chateau de Roscaër."

"Good God! Whatever for?"

"A picnic. Henri's coming too. I've asked Jacques, Christel and Monsieur Murchison."

"What, you know him?"

"But he's a lovely man. Ah! He keeps out of sight at the hotel, such a recluse. But we would just have to meet at the casino last night. Henri really liked him, he's thrilled with my idea. You can't imagine what the ruins of Roscaër are like in the moonlight. And there's going to be a wonderful moon tonight. So come on, lazybones."

Irène had already snatched the book away from me and was jokingly prodding me with her parasol like a matador's banderilla. I gave in, rather nonplussed. This gathering, this unexpected combination of people, I couldn't quite imagine it.

At five o'clock we gathered in the hotel garden. Irène, mightily pleased with herself, made the introductions. Allan was very elegant, very distant—absent. Christel, rather pale, put the food and the coats in the car. A strong wind was coming off the sea, blowing up an impressive storm in the upper branches of the larches and gigantic pines in the garden. Everyone bustled round rather frantically, made clumsy attempts to breathe life into a polite atmosphere that was too new, too questionable. At the sight of this impromptu group I suddenly got the feeling that the die was cast, that *these* were the ones who'd been chosen—that in an obscure way this ridiculous choice had committed us. It was as if I was looking at one of those photographs that *leap out* at you from the morning paper, where you see a front-page spread of a government minister who'd be killed in a plane crash a few minutes later, a group of climbers setting off only to be lost in an avalanche in the Alps.

But I'm being ridiculous. I probably caught it from Gregory, the superstitious Scotsman.

I went in Allan's car with Jacques. I don't know why but I remember that short trip as a long, long journey. Allan drove precisely, brusquely, with great style. His profile concentrated, taut. There was a solemnness about him. I watched those precise hands slipping speed into the slowness, the wrist with its leather bracelet gliding gently over the glowing instruments, and was suddenly seized by the haunting impression that I was next to a fighter pilot about to go in for the kill. No, he wouldn't bat an eyelid then either—and sitting beside him, neither would I. That fabulous, Indian, mask-like immobility that seems to be snatched constantly from a brief flash of lightning. He's definitely one of that great race of manhunters—the ones who can look anyone in the eye—at any time—as equals. A prince. A king.

No, Gregory's not so ridiculous after all.

The immobility of expression, the astounding angelic impassiveness of a man who, indifferently—*equally*—kills or saves: the surgeon bent over his scalpel, the soldier who plunges his blade into a strong chest. It's the same thing. Divine immobility. If these same hands, so nonchalantly expert, took it on themselves to throw me against that tree, at the crucial moment the eyes would give nothing away.

Once you pass Kérantec the road winds up steeply above the flat mirror of the sea. The sturdy skeleton of this cave-infested coast appears, its stretches of shore strung from point to point like hammocks, its white ripples, garlands of waves lingering as if spattered across a translucent background. Fine gauze cloud muffles the atmosphere—then comes the yellow gorse of the lower slopes, and suddenly the tunnel of a leafy, deserted forest, its floor bouncing beneath the raindrops. And always the high wind that wearies the heights so gloriously, the secret of forests by the sea, harmonized with the sea by the wind's musical fingers. It began to get dark, I was enjoying this escape beneath the low archway of leaves, raindrops showering down, where the soft sand of the verges was sprinkled with starry sun like light from semi-precious stones—an escape that makes you think of a journey from which there's no return. Passing through a forest is the only way I've ever imagined of getting to a mythical country. After that it's as if the scene is cleansed, becomes other, as if the open fields twinkle more lovingly in the faint light that rises beyond the twilight of branches.

As we came out of the forest, open moorland abruptly stretched away out of sight towards immense, mist-covered hills. In a fold in this bare terrain, like a vast yellow lawn of shimmering slopes, was a lake so perfectly clear, sheltered from the wind on this evening already dotted with stars, that it was as if we were entering an unknown, peaceful kingdom, amazingly tranquil, suddenly far from anything, leaf or branch, which might move or get alarmed. It was a true bowl, where your eye couldn't help but follow the gentle slope of the banks below the water—stately slopes broken here and there by low shingle walls. Alone on the shore of the lake, trees on a high rocky mound threw deep shadows, bristling among the beautiful flat surfaces that glowed like a well-groomed horse's coat, and then at the far end of the headland, in the hollow of this dead lake and at the edge of the mournful sky, all at once we saw the high walls of the Chateau de Roscaër.

The scene was so unexpectedly, so strangely beautiful that by unspoken agreement both cars stopped beside the lake, and for a while we sat in silence, absorbed by the sight. The steep slopes leading up to the ruins seemed to be covered with dense, dark forest, the tops of its unmoving greenery bristling with tiny bell towers and fanciful turrets—and from the top of these rocky prongs risen from the dark water, from the top of this prow dripping blood onto the sun through gaps in its ramparts, raised off the ground by a horizontal swathe of bluish mist from the lake, the edifice soared above the ages, became one of those *high places*, those ghostly peaks, inexpressibly pink, which rises above the clouds with the first stars as the sun goes down in the light from a different world.

We left the cars at the foot of the escarpment and began the climb. Christel, pale and slight, leaning on Allan's arm, went on ahead a hundred metres or so, and we often lost sight of them in the shadows of the enormous tree trunks. When they reappeared in a shaft of scattered light, and Allan pointed out an architectural detail on the gloomy towers whose tops kept looming out of the trees, a strange romantic engraving would suddenly appear to us, one of those distressed couples in a Gustave Doré who mysteriously wend their way like sleepwalkers in the moonlight towards a fortress as breathtakingly tall, as inaccessible as a magic mountain.

It's a very ancient ruin, completely overrun by plants and trees, an almost tropically lush vegetation that gathers stubbornly at the bottom of even the slightest gorge in Brittany. Great blankets of ground ivy, even the courtyard walls themselves bored out like well shafts, barely as wide, from where the perpetual night of the branches stretches out—literally *blocked* by an oak or a gigantic plane tree.

Sometimes a patch of bare wall, dizzying, terrible, shot up above a clump of trees.

Night fell as we finished eating. Here and there you could see the red glow of a cigarette. It was delightfully cool. Once the faces had disappeared, the voices produced a meticulously exact note, free of trickery, just the bare essentials. In the already less-comforting shadows Irène's artless effrontery toned down a little. How obvious it was that Allan intrigued her! She brought all her skill to bear to get information, cross-check his past—but Allan dodged the attack with superior effrontery. There was a distinct note of coldness in Christel's voice—this investigation, done publicly and so indiscreetly, so artlessly, and which she'd no doubt enjoyed carrying out by herself, *couldn't* possibly concern her. In the same way she seemed to take offence at the unsecretive, almost warm familiarity, the casual camaraderie that was suddenly revealed by Allan's and Jacques's conversation, so easily explained by their shared sporting interests. To Jacques there was clearly nothing *particularly* unusual in such a conversation by starlight in the grounds of an old chateau. He lacks a certain sixth sense, and although he'd been able to fool people up till then, in the rarefied and subtler atmosphere that was conspiring in the depths of this old chateau his wings failed him, he dropped like a stone. How could you not notice that Henri never misses an opportunity to contrast his own tone of voice with his wife's, to stress their essential difference at every moment, to join Allan and Christel on a quite different level—so much so that Irène gets annoyed. Among this little group, where the blur of the night, aroused curiosity, and for several days uneasiness has switched on a dormant electricity, a subtle polarity is developing, attractions are taking shape, shocking, unexpected, sudden—this vague tangle of human beings is coming apart as if in an electrified bath. And beneath the smiling, trivial words of the conversation a magic mirror could suddenly show me Jacques disguised as the village idiot, a frenzied Iréne, red with rage and scornful vulgarity, giving themselves away, getting muddled, lost at the sight of this unexpected alliance, these impenetrable judges' faces in whose shadow Henri, Christel, Allan must be standing—in that confused half-light where you can vaguely sense the hand of Fate.

I only remember the rest of the evening in hazy views, where a gesture, a word has sometimes frozen in my memory forever. Although actually what was there about that walk that wasn't normal? But when I go back over it I find my memory cluttered with childish flirtations. And besides, the night was so beautiful, so wild. The couples hover—as closed off, as secretly harmonious as astral spheres—around the ancient ramparts of the castle, like in the garden scene in *Faust*. Like a comet with its fiery tail Allan picks off the slower stars along his overpowering course. A process of decantation is at work—in the calm of the night, soothed, everyone's breathing goes back to normal.

Again I see Allan and Christel walking slowly along the highest rampart in the castle. Moonlight searches that celestial face which you find on trees in high places at night, that enraptured, motionless face like someone sleeping out *under the stars*. The startling light of the lake in the darkness, like pale morning held prisoner under the ice—the clearness of large expanses of still water even on the darkest nights—clearings in the quiet night.

Allan is talking about nocturnal landscapes that have struck him—an Asiatic peak he saw by moonlight during a trip to the Indies, suddenly, from the bottom of a valley hidden beneath trees—a great palish-blue triangle, final, its tip just appearing out of the black of the night—and simply from the effort of looking up to study its frightening bearing you suddenly felt yourself go pale. "I was suddenly convinced that a *thing* like that couldn't have appeared from the ground, quite the opposite, it had been *placed* there under cover of darkness—dropped from above—there was such a radical connection between the earth and this apocalyptic sign. I think there's a Jules Verne story about the moon that comes too close to the earth and leaves a piece of mountain stuck on it as it goes past. That was what it was."

He'd clambered playfully onto the top of the wall and accompanies us from there, on the edge of the precipice like a spirit, defying all fear of heights. He delights in talking to us now, casually and subtly, enjoying our angry discomfort at the risks he's taking. We daren't ask him to come down: unrestrained, wild, capricious, suddenly we have a sense of him *as he really is*, in the grip of his demons, clad in a protective taboo. His sharp eye settles on Christel, on me—this is definitely the jaguar that Gregory talked about, motionless on his branch. This individual is so obviously a provocation, he fascinates. But

Christel can't resist the unbearable challenge—she jumps onto the wall next to him, and he follows her, deferential, protective, slightly ironic—and, at last released, I can ask them to stop their cruel game.

"Do you like the night, Christel?"

"Yes, I love it. Sometimes so much that I can't rest easy in my room. Last night I was listening to the great volleys of the tide rising in the bay, beneath a black night sky without stars. It seemed as if the water was dissolving the night—that it was rising, rising, besieging my room, the balcony I lean on like a gangway in a shipwreck. I was almost frightened. And then I had a strange dream, very much related to what I'd just been thinking about. I was in the balcony of a theatre half-flooded with violent waves. The boxes were streaming with water, it splashed up as if they were little skiffs, the way coasts full of caves frolic unexpectedly in the spray, and, soaked, freezing, I felt the same pleasure as a child who runs in front of breaking waves—and there I was in raptures, leaning on the red balustrade, watching the waves rush over the stage, in an extraordinary state of expectation. Eventually a wave formed, swelled, rose to the flies: a magnificent mountain of water. With fantastic suction the auditorium emptied as it approached; you could see the seats in the stalls, firmly fixed to the floor, re-emerging from the deep with a wooshing of water being drawn up. The bigger the wave grew the larger the theatre became, rising to the clouds and, the only one left on board the sinking auditorium like the captain of a ship, for a second I had a vertical wall of smooth black water hanging in front of me, bursting with seething silvery bubbles. My fear turned to wild delight, unbounded hope. The more the wave advanced—a wave whose reality, whose exhilarating weight, so imminent, so close, was already making my shoulders give way—the more my confidence, the boundless sense of security I now felt, pierced it, dissolved it. It seemed to become strangely transparent—behind it, deep in the water, stars were shining as softly, as peacefully as over the deserts of Egypt before the promised land. And as I was engulfed, carried away forever, weak as a feather, I realized this wave was the same as the night.

"But I really do love it. I especially enjoy watching it fall on summer evenings in a big city. The café terraces suddenly empty—what's happening? The boulevards attract me especially with their endless misty yellow views where the trams get bigger, motionless like a ship coming in from the open sea, decked out with flags as if back from the firing line, laden with branches and flowers with the strange scent of an exotic forest. Because of this hesitant dusk, this giddiness, this drowsiness, the heartbreaking, cello-like scraping as the rails go round a corner—I've often thought that trees are overrunning the suburbs, surrounding the city with a forest with no way out. I used to enjoy disappearing into leafy avenues at twilight, that advance guard that thrusts into the city's threatened heart (because one day the city will be conquered by trees). Soon the traffic gets less and less then dies out completely—you make your way along dumbstruck, yawning streets. Particularly near railway stations—night comes so quickly from out of those great piles of coal.

94

Then, at liberty, branches slip gently over the ill-kept walls of private houses—it's the suburbs already. At last here are some hedges, fields with rivers running through them; there's no question of knowing where to go now. Once past houses where familiar night falls so quickly you notice there's still a little daylight left. You can never tell when it's actually dark.

"The average person has amazingly little experience of the night. Just as they're probably too suspicious of this unexpected source of advice to listen to any pearls of wisdom it might have to offer them, no doubt the only image of the tomb they're prepared to accept is the one they see around them in their bedroom, with its furniture and flowers, full of *doubles* like those underground burial chambers in Ancient Egypt. Maybe they're afraid that if they slept in the open air they'd wake up to find they were lost—because to my mind you don't shut yourself away just because you're afraid of common thieves. There was a time when I preferred sleeping in places where night seemed to fall in a particularly pure state: churches, public parks."

We'd reached the corner of the chateau, which jutted out over the lake like a belvedere. Thick vegetation surged up the feathery battlements, walling them in, turning them into a secret hiding place where, in the moonlight, a walnut tree threw complex, ocellated shadows as black as Indian ink. Above us the walls of a tower, silky-smooth, glowing gently, completely *bathed* in light, leapt up into the cold brightness of the breathtaking night. A cool breeze came from the lake. In a distant village a church clock struck eleven, summoning up a host of metaphors from childhood compositions, and Allan smiled:

"I think it was when I was a student that I discovered a passion for churches at night. There's nothing easier than getting yourself locked in—in country churches especially, the people are pretty trusting. Nowadays, as Wilde would say, no one steals sacred objects anymore. Needless to say this fad (to be honest there was more than a touch of that in it) had nothing of the sacrilegious, still less of mystic exultation—it was just that I'd always thought that at dusk it had to be more *revealing* than any other place."

At this point something Gregory said in his letter came back to me unexpectedly, although hazily—like two sets of clues might tie up in a detective's mind when it's still not quite clear how they tally—and I pricked up my ears.

"For a long time, once the door had been locked behind me and I was alone in the great nave, bathed in rich pools of sunlight through the stained glass, listening to birds sing outside the windows, watching the branches move, I was overcome by languor in my imprisonment, anxiety, a sudden mad desire to rush through fields and meadows in broad daylight. But now as twilight approached the holy dread returned. It's then that you have to have heard, in this nave with its tomb-like echoes, outside those windows, blind like panes of frosted glass, and those smells that speak so directly to your soul in a church—candles, cold flagstones, and the extraordinary sweetness of lilies in the half-light—the sounds of the day dying one by one, that silence with which churches are always brimming, growing, gathering, really *taking shape* like a wave rises from the trough that comes before it. Oh! The last birdsong, the last sound, so slow to die out—taken up again, maintained for endless heroic intervals—whose far-distant, nostalgic, pointless convulsions I could hear fading away—that utterly lost, meditative sweetness! Then came the wind's last bow-strokes on the leaves, solemn, as final as a *petite mort*, definitely the last sigh of the day—and finally silence. An invisible tidying up, rather like getting ready for bed, takes place in a structure that's casting off for the night crossing—and I sometimes felt uncomfortable at the familiarity of this yawning silence around the sacred, as if I could see an invisible woman keeping vigil over her dead child; and yet she's walking, coughing, she's even eating. And so silence set in, a silence made up of creaking chairs and the more and more haunting sputtering of candles—a silence that began with gentle little noises at twilight but which now, the paler the windows became, took on a strange magnitude. And now night settled in with its great black expanses, and suddenly everything changed perspective. The candles! That mystic portcullis they bring down in front of an altar lost in darkness, sometimes a statue revealed by a stronger play of light, as if behind some unreal grove swept by the glow of a Bengal candle—the gentle, trembling death of the flame at the very tip, that dizzying thread sunk deep in the darkness—how greedily, how fervently I gazed at it for hours on end. Flame with the black heart where violent heat, the spearhead and the aspen leaf take refuge like in the belly of a woman, tireless little light—so motionless, so dormant that you imagine it rising from the bottom of the deepest well of darkness—like the softened reflection of a tongue of fire in mystic waters. Something fascinated me, something inside me which had just burnt itself on this light like a moth. It wasn't the fire on a night in the country, which makes you think of supper and bed, it was more like a light on the surface of the water which casts spells on chasms, wards off the irrevocable. Sometimes I became so deeply absorbed in this vision, like they say the yogi do in India, that I really became that flame, felt its light feeding on my heart. Ah! If only it could have dissolved me, melted and sprinkled me, light and fluid as the air, cold as the flagstones, among the cool swimming spaces of these tall dark archways, forever at rest. An odd phrase came to me, which I repeated ad nauseam as if it contained some magic power: it lies with that flame alone to restore the night to us. Ah! If only the night could have hollowed out, sunk down, dealt with the glimmer of the candles—ah, if only daylight hadn't returned! Hours passed like minutes. And then so soon it was dawn, and suddenly the dark vaults were covered with large blue-grey patches, muted as shadows and as if cut from the same cloth. And it was morning again."

Hearing a slight rustle of leaves I turned and saw Irène had silently joined us, had probably been listening to Allan for the last few minutes. The childish complicity that had bound the three of us together in the dead of night, and now suddenly allowed to speak its mind, was about to be broken. There was no mistaking the tone of Irène's voice.

"How very odd, highly romantic even. But you haven't said what you were looking for in that church."

"Isn't that maybe an indiscreet question?"

"So what kind of sanctuary are you looking for in the night? I was almost about to believe you were talking seriously. Are you really so mistrustful of being awake? Of *real* life? Although you seem to know how to turn it to your advantage quite nicely."

There was rising hostility in her voice.

"I may have known how to make the most of life—I've no regrets about that. But I don't think it means I'm not allowed to be interested in its opposite side."

"That amazes me coming from you. Is death something worth thinking about? It's going to happen without you anyway. What a childish and demeaning way of thinking, so pointless."

"Fair point. But you seem to be *unaware of*—you seem to *ignore*—(an inflexion in Allan's voice played on the English meaning—*to ignore*) a possible objection—death can be a deliberate act. Seen from that angle the perspectives change."

"Just what do you mean exactly?"

"That we can also kill ourselves. As soon as we're able to think of death as an act, a conquest, when we're conscious of having that right, we can challenge certain inhibitions that apply in every other case. *From then on* why stand on ceremony?"

"So have you decided to 'have done with life'?"

Despite Irène's mockery the conversation had taken such a sudden, silly turn that I felt most uneasy. It looked (was it a trick of the light, that mercurial moon shining through the black branches?) as if Christel, silent, staring fixedly, had suddenly gone pale. Casually, with a peculiar smile like a poker player who's holding an invisible card, Allan said:

"In any case, dear lady, I wouldn't be so indiscreet as to talk about it in such esteemed company."

The night had turned chilly. We walked back down under the great trees. I could feel Christel's arm trembling beneath mine—from cold? From irritation? Loud, good-natured shouts drifted up to us from the bottom of the hill, punctuated by a car horn. In the light from the headlights Henri and Jacques were waiting, slapping themselves rhythmically to keep warm.

29th July

WHEN I GOT UP THIS MORNING I suddenly felt the miraculous presence of autumn at the heart of summer, like fruit feels the bite of the worm that kills it. Over this day, mild, still warm, with that wonderful hazy light (yet with something slightly on the wane, slightly distant: the gossamer fineness of a beautiful face at the onset of consumption) there was a great rush of fresh air, steady, healthy, bracing—a suddenly perceptible clear space, like something you could drink, absorb—one of those purely spatial sensations in the hollow of your chest, the fullest and most intoxicating of all in which beauty becomes pure *inspiration*, and which you can tell from a certain unnatural puffing out of the chest like in an ancient figure of Victory. Long halcyon days that lull you night after night like a hammock, face constantly turned away from the too-nostalgic, too-tender sky—days swept away like palms on an atoll, dissolved and unresisting in a great terrestrial flood of elemental freshness—days of foreboding, of wings spreading, mysterious farewells, vague prophecies, of divine, delicate lightness almost dying of golden ripeness, to the point of pain, *well-being*, a smile senseless with the sweetness of waves, open sea, to the point of lethargy, to the point of fascination. Ah! Nothing but sand, sea—the heavenly transparency of day, that boundless parabola to infinity, that soft radiant mist that pierces the heart from *elsewhere*—like a sacrifice to the mortal beauty of day, like a poet's premonition, the vague summons of winter mists in the hollows of this heavenly softness, faint trails of smoke from the channels left by seaweed fishermen's boats.

And yet I'm in no mood to enjoy this heartbreaking beauty unthinkingly. I'm not really at peace with myself—all out of tune. Yesterday in the heat of the afternoon I found myself wandering the corridors of the hotel like a lost soul that can't find its resting place. That walk the other day, I still have a mellow, moon-like, even poetic impression of it. I listened to those two well-matched voices alternating in the darkness—it had the atmosphere of a childhood dream about it, an abandon that I enjoyed immensely. Yet there's a riddle that's annoying me—a problem to which I don't have the key. Something's going on here. What bothers me about all these episodes over the last few days, outwardly so insignificant—the ones I've confided to this journal—this is how I'd attempt to describe them: in the gestures, the words, there's admittedly been no sign of anything that isn't totally *plausible*, nothing that could seem the least bit odd to anyone with a cool head—and yet at every moment the reactions of all those involved, of me myself (and from whom could I judge better?) have seemed to go way beyond what those gestures, those insignificant words are able to bear out. As if—in the same way a theme buried in an orchestra and running beneath the thread of a melody sometimes disrupts it, suddenly enriches, solemnizes it, gives it mellowness, resonance, a sudden pulse of innuendo—an unknown *motif* seemed to continue the sentences after the voices stopped speaking, the gestures after the hand stopped moving, transposing these trivial episodes into a much more dynamic key. And if this motif really exists, it's Allan who holds the secret to it.

I'm sure he and Irène parted as enemies at Roscaër. They clashed like people from different races. And most likely the hostilities won't end there.

How suddenly everything around me on the beach has lost its colour! Those innocent holiday pleasures, the snort of the animal running free in the meadows, my heart's not in it anymore. Gregory's letter played a nasty trick on me. After Dolorés left I was ready to turn my back on these ghosts who might have needed all my efforts to bring them to life. And now it's given me back a kind of importance—it's entrusted me with a mission. It's amazing to think just how far you can *involve* someone in a situation, even the most repellent, the most thankless, just by persuading them of the decisive importance their participation could have. Personal advantage probably counts for little in motivating people—but their ever-alert dramatic instinct, now there's a motive that virtually never fails to respond to an appeal. Perhaps people are always vaguely dreaming of *giving a star performance* some day or other. Sometimes during lunch, foolishly, I look at Allan and put my hand in the pocket where I keep Gregory's letter—and I feel such low-grade pleasure, yet as much determination as a policeman who's tailing a crook. No doubt I've allowed myself to become taken with it—and here I am watching, waiting, on the lookout for an event that I find myself almost wishing will happen, whatever the outcome.

And who can say I'm the only one here? Who can say how far the person who begins *to be taken with it* will be driven? There's a paper still waiting to be written on the birth of tragedy, quite different from Nietzsche's. However far back you go, even in the most well-constructed, the soundest, most securely-seated on the 'passions', you can be sure that somewhere in the plot there's always an unjustifiable urge in one of the characters, a sudden inspiration as violent as a change in the wind, which deep down can't be justified by any motive except a sudden desire, an irresistible impulse to throw their weight on the scales, use up their dramatic *virtue* that very moment whatever the cost, and for no better reason than to get on wholeheartedly with the game. Yes, at the theatre I've often thought of tragedy in that way: a form of holy madness, an infectious state of trance, a solstice bonfire that spreads from one character to the next. "Ah! Now we'll see. Me too, me too … !" Like an athlete can't set foot on the track without all the others longing to join the race.

But there are ways and ways of playing. A special birthright gives a man like Allan the position of king of the theatre: he's a lord, a prince of life. I sense I'm only cut out—at best—for the role of confidant. Why at every opportunity I get to push myself forward do I feel I have to withdraw like this? This need to hide behind another person, to follow in someone's wake—I've never been able to shake it off. Perhaps I gain greater perceptiveness from it—or at least imagine I do. But maybe that's wrong. Maybe it's just a totally harmless, totally innocent reaction to my own decline. There's a natural system of compensation by which anyone in an inferior position imagines— maybe through a greater sense of detachment—that he *understands* better, has mastered his part better. There's not one manservant who at the slightest lapse in professional discretion doesn't feel authorized to tell his master what to do. Not a single clerk who doesn't spend all day picking holes in the minister's plans.

Yet maybe that would be the one unredeemable crime—in a wasted life whittled and gnawed away by sloth, fear, that meticulous calculator. The painstaking daily destruction of possibilities. And to put an end to everything, that smothering process justified by a cosy regime of scepticism. What begins as: '*I make a point of being unpleasant deliberately for fear of being unpleasant naturally*', (Mauriac) continues with: "*I make a point of failing deliberately for fear of failing naturally*", and which could eventually finish up as: "I make a point of dying deliberately for fear of dying naturally" (a superbly comic line). Perhaps no neater way of using up your life than with such a combination of arrogance and cowardice ('*It'll finish badly*').

These last few days Henri and I have got to know each other much better. I've got some little confidences out of him, which confirm what I thought I noticed from the start—his barely perceptible clash with Irène. He clearly sidelines her somewhat, but there's a vitality, an energy about her which keeps up appearances and only much later betrays the cracks that would already be beginning to appear on the face of a less energetic woman. But in contrast, being generous by nature, she has thrown herself into a whirl of dancing, sport, social frenzy, like a thoroughbred whose first reaction to an injury is to dash off at a gallop. She sulks with skill—and it so happens that Jacques, the indecisive, easily influenced young man, isn't totally indifferent to this sudden outburst of vitality. On the beach, on the tennis court, at afternoon assignation time at the casino I seem to see them together rather more than usual. Perhaps some vague memory of that evening at Roscaër has a hand in it? They found themselves on the same side of the fence.

I watched them dancing at the casino last night, in that beautiful aquarium light of spot lamps projected onto the ceiling like rockets, and broken up by the Baudelairean sounds of the saxophone (yes, why not: '*That trumpet's sound is so magnificent*') in a form of tropical undergrowth lit by great whorls of flower petals. Something of the theatre's floodlit darkness finds its way into pleasure spots along with the insidious lighting, which gives even commonplace beauty a brief halo, an accent, a little depth. They're both good-looking and danced well together—without the least self-consciousness, you'd probably have imagined—yet I sensed (they saw me) that in this proud jousting, this ritual strutting, in an obscure way they were seeking—all the while moving so contemptuously, so imperviously—a kind of revenge, to trample down some vague embarrassment, a humiliation.

Now and then I imagined (but could you trust yourself in the deceptive flicker of the lights) that surreptitiously they were looking for a sign of admiration, approval in my eyes, which—so childishly—would have *cleared their debts*. Or to be more precise (I'm thinking of Irène), avenged them.

Since the going of Gregory, who had a soft spot for miniature golf, Henri and I have got back to serious golf, and like to start the day with a round on those peaceful mornings when you look out at a sea still sleepy from the night. Yesterday as we were finishing our round and heading back to the clubhouse, I mentioned to Henri how much the greens, with the lush good health of salt meadows, reminded me of the surprising, tawny fur on the hills around Roscaër. I noticed a sudden faint flicker of interest on Henri's face, as if some tiny object, a grain of sand, had struck him between the eyes.

"It was a pretty strange evening wasn't it, Henri?"

"Yes. And a bit crazy. It's just like Irène to come up with such ill-matched gatherings—incoherent."

There was a note of irritation in his voice, but the word struck me with its unintentional accuracy. So I wasn't alone in feeling that way! It seemed best to stick to generalities.

"It's odd to hear you use that expression. For someone who weighs their words, as you and I are occasionally capable of doing, you do realize it takes us back to the question of elective affinities?"

107

Henri gave me a pointed look. We both sensed we were starting to 'take short cuts'.

"Maybe. So let's assume Irène is an intrepid experimenter, not even afraid there might be an explosion. You'll agree that's exactly how we make discoveries."

Something in his voice made me think he was applying this last expression to himself in particular.

"My dear Henri, what some people call an innocent taste for experiments, others have sometimes called 'tempting fate'. The Church doesn't have a great liking for alchemists. Although what did they do if not investigate basic attractions? What a lovely temptation, so straightforward! Mix fire and water, salt and sulphur. That's how you cheerfully cast out demons. Yet I'm sure what guided them was just an unbridled appetite for universal friendship."

"All these polite chemical metaphors of yours make Irène sound like some kind of procurer. You're being pretty harsh, Gérard."

"But don't you think that one way or other everyone would like to be a procurer. Putting two substances, two people together and seeing if they explode or mix. It's quite natural."

"And perhaps perverse."

"Nature is perverse! The human race is perverse! Luckily. It's how things get done. It's how people meet, and every opportunity, everything new comes from that. How could things and individuals make contact, enrich each other, without *perverting* them, without diverting them from the safe, well-trodden path, without new ideas? Whether that's the work of the devil or not, agree on everything else. The devil is a diversion—he's always *oblique*."

For a moment Henri was lost in thought.

"Perhaps. But to get back to the elective affinities, all the same I don't think (yet his voice was serious, on some deeper level at odds with his friendly objection—yes, there was even a touch of anxiety) you take that old joke seriously. Goethe dug it up from the bottom of the fireplace in the boudoir of the Age of Enlightenment to amuse himself. And, I might add, he made a pretty tedious novel out of it."

"My dear Henri, I'm not taking sides in the debate. But after all, maybe psychology isn't confident enough to dump that sentimental view of the world of the soul back in the distant past (I was being as ironic as I could). Chemistry has taken the place of alchemy, there's no doubt about that. Fine. But as for psychology, romantic psychology I mean, to my mind it's not its practical success (however could it express itself?), in the end it's social pressure that acts as the judge of theories. I've no idea what it's *worth*—probably no more or less than anything else—but my point is that Goethe's idea didn't get a chance because society couldn't give it one without sparking off a chain of disasters. You can imagine this stormy world, shot through with the constant glow of love at first sight, soulmates migrating like wild ducks, couples made and unmade, a ballet of iron filings around the magnet. It was simply unacceptable. The world of the perpetual trance. You've got to admit that the much-vaunted idea of crystallization served the purposes of the social hypocrisy

109

of marriage, or the decent liaison if you like, in other ways. And how successfully! In fact it was Stendhal, the false anarchist, who gave marriage according to the Code its mythical basis afterwards. Having borrowed its style he owed it that, as the textbooks say."

I was pleased with my little speech, although, amused at first, Henri seemed to become thoughtful.

"Perhaps you're right. Some people are better off dead. Even in the Code Goethe gets his revenge; it really makes you think."

"What are you referring to?"

"That wonderful instance where divorce is due to 'mutual incompatibility'. It would have delighted your alchemists."

I felt like making a joke to divert a conversation which, given its apparently harmless subject matter, was far too strained, and whose slightly forced repartee wasn't innocent.

We walked on along the cliff in silence, drawn by the bleak, flat expanses that stretched towards the open countryside. The land here comes down to the sea more decorously than elsewhere, without trees, without that crazy costume of fertile land—like two beautiful bodies undressing before they make love, out of a greater sense of ceremony. Henri told me how much this destitution attracted him. I'd never have suspected this moderate and seemingly shy man of harbouring a taste for limitless horizons. We were alone in the depths of the listless, sleepy morning; to a late stroller using the telescope on the esplanade, two tiny black dots, two insects making their way across a blanket.

"Have you ever noticed," Henri asked me out of the blue, "that at certain times of life dreams come back to us barely altered, all linked by a significant detail like a resemblance in family portraits?"

"I don't dream very often so I don't get much chance to notice sequences like that. But I think it happens to nearly everyone. It happened to me when I was younger."

"I'm probably getting younger then. Several times during the last fortnight I've had the same dream, definitely the same. One of those rare dreams, structured, insistent, as if organized round a dominant theme and which stays in your memory long after you've woken up, till late in the day. With something of the warning about it—I wouldn't go so far as to call it significant— something that quite unaccountably *concerns* me. Perhaps you remember in Dostoyevsky, the beginning of *The Eternal Husband:* several times, several days running, the hero Veltchaninov bumps into a man in the busy street, a perfectly ordinary man as it happens, whose face vaguely reminds him of something. That's all. Gradually his life changes, his health deteriorates, he feels totally distraught, totally confused. I can vouch for my pulse being perfectly normal—but there's something of that in my recurring dream."

"You're making me curious."

"What keeps coming back so insistently in this dream is a landscape. I'm on a high plateau, a vast area that stretches as far as the eye can see with long green grass, dark-green grass rippling like the sea, whose even swell vanishes over the horizon in great sheets. Above

111

me a magnificent blue sky with a great array of heavy cumulus, like celestial white horses, which disappear into the middle distance along with the rippling grass. The movement of the clouds traces an angle in the sky whose point makes an apex and, like a perfect reflection in a mirror of water, the shimmering flight of the sea of grass also converges onto this same mysterious point in one great angle. In broad daylight (the sun is magnificent, glorious, unbearable) it's like one of those pictures of the sunset by naive painters where a fan of red rays across both the sky and the sea (a fan unlike any in real life) expresses an unusual obsession with embodied perspective, raised to the level of potent ghost, ghoul, absorbent, draining a landscape of its substance towards a *vanishing point* like the tentacle of a magnetic field whose power of suction suddenly becomes the head of a torrent, the eye of a maelstrom. The wind on my face, breathtaking, pure, dizzyingly cool, intoxicates like wine, suggests limitless altitude, something like the páramo of the Andes, the high places of the Pamirs, triggering a wild desire to consume this expanse, to race to the horizon with it across this ocean of grass, this carpet of celestial seaweed, these glacier sargassos.

"Near me on my left, opposite the vanishing point, the plateau finishes abruptly, cut off by a frightening cliff. Beside this vast smooth plateau, as naked and majestic as a planet, the chasm—carved out, excavated, full of cavities—looks like the bottom of an upturned diamond mine, a saw-cut through a termites' nest. To be precise it reminds you of those cardboard human figures with movable joints in natural science departments, where here and there you can peel off the smooth layer that represents the skin, and a multicoloured maze of veins, nerves and intestines suddenly appears, as disconcerting and unsavoury as a seething horde of red ants under a paving stone. The phenomenal distance to the bottom of the abyss gives it that bluish tint you see in the distance in great river valleys at nightfall. Stretching away at the bottom, as clear as through a naval telescope, is a familiar human landscape, a tangle of trees, wayward paths, houses with gardens, all so tiny, rivers, the outskirts of a city with the gentle smoke of the suburbs.

"With surprising clarity, sharpness, I gaze into these mysterious city streets. There's an early evening atmosphere, golden sunlight on greasy pavements damp from a recent shower, the sparkle of wet stone, the cheerful bustle of closing time. I'm overcome by inexpressible emotion at every trifling detail: a kerb, an empty, sleepy street—it's so confusing to see it from above, stretched out just a stone's throw away from a teeming avenue—the comings and goings outside a big hotel, peaceful trees in a public garden—and I don't know why, a tremendous sense of love. For me there's something overwhelming, breathtaking about feeling I'm here alone, watching this town from unseen heights like a soaring eagle, a god, as if in thrall to the devil on the mountain top—this defenceless city, so fragile, as if held by a claw in the midst of an extraordinary calm. Not a breath of wind—then a slight mist comes down—for a moment the distance reappears as if swept along by a river, so incredibly flimsy, dissolved, wistful in the deep shadows of its trees, and the vision disappears. With the rising mist from the chasm the plateau closes like a sliding door at the mouth of the fissure, and the wilderness of grass stretches away to the horizon again."

30th July

I WAKE THIS MORNING—is it the after-effect of Henri's dream?—full of the buzzings and murmurings of a journey. Intoxicating memories come back to me from far away, from the depths of childhood; memories of setting off—and for me it was nearly always setting off for a beach like this one, so much are the smells of trains and sunshine connected. Again I see the cavernous half-light beneath the high glass roof, I hear the excited uproar of engines suddenly echoing under the arches, halting breathlessly like the beast in its lair, the dragon's cave. At the far end below a glass panel that half-blocks the exits, in a glorious blaze of sunshine, deep in a cutting with houses high above it I see the rails flowing away, an image of infinity for me alone. The dark smell of coal adds its warmth to that of the fresh brioches and the great showers of sun pouring over the tracks, and I remember the engine sheds too, the blast furnaces, jackhammers, everything dedicated to the mystery of fire. Nearby, in hollows in the stone walls the waiting-rooms are cool as caves; the *perfect phrases*—completely self-sustaining, hanging in the air like diamond chandeliers from an archway—of those mysterious posters come back to my heart. '*Port-Vendres, the shortest and most sheltered crossing*', '*The chateau and village of Beynac*', or even '*Fantômas luxury cruises*', with, above a dark green headland tipped with slender pines plunging down to a petrol blue sea, the single mysterious name, as if needing no further explanation: '*Formentor*'. Yes, those station exits, black channels still full of traces of sparks from the smokestack and the smell of sulphur, it's now, faced with my unruly desires, beside this meandering ocean, that a *pressure pipeline* stretches out before me, flowing lazily as a river across a plain.

That's what Allan has become for me, for us, I sense it now.

3rd August

S O THE SEASON is in full swing. New faces appear at the hotel. And yet they won't be anything to me, I know it. My holiday world will stay confined to that small, chance group of people, the ones my memory will always associate, come what may, with the most unusual *initiation*. Whatever part chance played in this choice—whatever absurd part—it would be pointless trying to prove it to me. Chance is a deity—more complex, more exacting, more secretive than any other. With Henri, with Irène, Jacques, even with Gregory if he comes back I feel the same bond as with a group of people who had their baptism of fire at the same time as me. I know this language is excessive, these notes incommunicable—but this language, these notes are just for me. "I was setting my fever down on paper."

There's nothing that people rebel more against, I told Jacques, than being forced to acknowledge the secret and immediate power their fellow human beings have over them. There's maybe nothing more common, routine. A savage power, as indifferent as a thunderbolt, where intellect, merit, beauty, language are nothing but animal electricity, a polarity that suddenly develops. Falling under the spell. Forever. We never talk about it—it's taboo. Yet many many years later in the course of a con-

117

versation, at a mere inflection of the voice, at eyes suddenly averted, initiates will suddenly recognize an angel's passing, that sudden shared revelation, love at first sight: '*God will recognize his angels by an inflection in their voice and their secret regrets*'. It seems the Christian mystery that people find easiest to understand through personal experience is the Visitation. Antiquity, always so welcoming, so quick to see the god in a chance visitor, spared itself by way of a good healthy miracle—yes, perhaps the *worst* of misunderstandings.

In the days when a stranger might
be mistaken for a god in disguise,
there was a knock at the door.

4th August

N O, GREGORY WASN'T MISTAKEN. My premonitions weren't mistaken. I now have a fact to add to Allan's case, a fact that's unfortunately all too certain.

Last night Christel was so especially insistent about dragging me off to the casino that in the end I went, thinking that all she wanted me for was as an alibi so she wouldn't look too helpless in front of Allan. It was the *première* of some film that had recently been made in the area. At the far end of the room whose open verandas look onto the beach, the screen was stretched out with the sea behind it, a horizon already dotted with stars and the beams of lighthouses, its dancing images occasionally moving in the fitful sea breeze. Out to sea the night was so luminous, so glorious, so seemingly endless that they decided to delay the showing and, like the black sail of a ghost ship, the screen hung there for some time with its back to an incandescent, pearly sea which wouldn't fade away. Quietly we got ice creams, coats pulled up over our knees like blankets against the stirrings of cool night air, as if on the deck of transatlantic liner. The same self-consciousness we'd felt at Kérantec returned to haunt us. That same insurmountable wall; our fate was sealed. We probably haven't been able to do anything for each other for quite a while now. Suddenly beset by blind compassion, certain that on a magnificent still night like this the gesture *couldn't* be misinterpreted, I took Christel's hand for a moment, like you hold a sick person's feverish hand during a bad attack just to say: "I'm here". She looked at me unsurprised, a look so remote, so inaccessible, and I think I heard her murmur: "What's the use?" I noticed she was wearing a faded scarf round her neck, pale, unusual, a luxurious heavy fabric, dignified as if made from the silk of an ancient flag. Upright beside me in the half-darkness she suddenly represented the inexplicable approach of a dream; one of those statues that suddenly land beside us, appear from some backward glance we give when we feel an insistent gaze on us, and stare dreamily, fixedly over our shoulder at a point on the horizon.

During the interval I left Christel for a moment and went to the gaming rooms—fascinated as ever by the brusque ceremonial, the bare impoverishment of the setting which gives off waves of overly intense emotions in all directions: an operating theatre, a circus, an amphitheatre. In front of me I suddenly saw Allan. And from the expressions of the other players, a certain feverish concentration, the suddenly frozen faces of various onlookers passing through during the interval, I immediately realized that something out of the ordinary was happening.

Distracted, slightly sleepy, eyes blurred—his expression is so familiar to me already—drumming his fingers lightly on the edge of the green baize table, at each spin of the wheel Allan spread out in front of him—anywhere, to the left, the right, with an indifference that couldn't have been an act, with the mechanical regularity of an engine driver shovelling fuel into a boiler—a mass of chips which at first glance seemed exorbitant. The seven, the eight, then the ten, the three: with sudden leaps, changes, incomprehensible jerks, as if more than the outcome of his bet, he was looking out for certain intersecting lines and numbers, for the answer to some obscure algebraic problem (I thought of the problem of the knight in chess: "He's trying close the circle".) He lost regularly—and judging by the looks from his opponents the total already swallowed up must have been enormous. I noticed that before he spun the ball the croupier shot him a quick anxious glance, almost undetectable, hidden behind that professional dispassion which can spot the marked man out of a thousand at Monte Carlo, the one picked out that same evening for the bad cheque or the bullet. An unbearable dismayed embarrassment began to set in round the table. Behind me I heard someone mutter under their breath: "He's mad." So obviously, conspicuously, so outrageously was he playing *against himself*, lost in a fever where speed itself gave his gestures that absurd insouciance, that slowness—that nearby I sensed mouths panting with primitive tension, ready to cry out: "Enough! Enough!"—fists clenched as if to overturn the table, to stop this nightmare, this suffocation. Eyes half-closed, smiling loftily, Allan took delight in their wild eyes, their cruel stares, their hands kneading together, tormenting this room that he was dangling at his fingertips. The sight of the mesmerized crowd, suddenly seen in the mirror, was extraordinary. It was as obvious as when from a riverbank you see a drowning man go under, that this was a man lost—and, offensively, impertinently, mercilessly, he was taking his time over it, arranging it in clever stages, removing the veils of benign, bland, mollifying assumptions one by one and standing upright in the unbearable and now indisputable nakedness of scandal, he *was forcing everyone to guess what his game was.*

There was one awful moment. One by one almost every player stopped placing bets, presumably refusing to think of even vaguely collaborating in what was about to happen *here*. A circle of terrible, imploring, furious eyes now besieged Allan, shooting him at point-blank range, virtually smothering him, cutting off his retreat, calling down thunder and lightning or a flood, denying this suffocating scene any chance of a normal outcome *now*. As he was about to spin the ball the croupier paused—I think the little scene lasted two or three seconds—and looked Allan in the eye, and suddenly everyone sensed they were on the brink of what was bearable, the precise instant when this heart-rending tension refused to get any worse, and would annihilate, expel him. I was torn. I *had* to do something, stop this dizzy fever, this climax.

I touched Allan on the shoulder.

"Allan! You're crazy!"

He turned round, totally relaxed, horrifyingly composed.

"What's going on?"

He followed me with a shrug, smiling now, spiritual, eloquent, so relaxed that suddenly I felt ridiculous. I took him into the darkened garden. So calm, so well-behaved! Like a friend you've just seen bleeding to death in a nightmare and who you wake up to find smiling, frivolous, lively, quite oblivious to any danger. His high spirits were infectious. I no longer knew—but would I ever know—*what I was dealing with*. What do I say to him from now on?

After the interval I went back to Christel.

"I bumped into Allan. He was playing for high stakes."

"Oh really?"

So insipid, so colourless was the picture I painted for her in such a trite way that I was actually relieved she reacted so casually; and I even managed to find the rest of the evening bearable.

Thank God!—she didn't *see*.

6th August

I 'M STRUGGLING to stir up a mass of miserable, stagnant thoughts. Outside the lowered blinds the sound of the sea and the crowds on the beach make a remorseless rumbling in the sweltering sun, like the monotonous roar of a ferocious crowd in an amphitheatre. Now and then the wood panelling creaks in the heat. A ray of sunlight quivers in an elaborate swirl of dust, a plumed cascade of sun. I yawn sluggishly, haggard, relaxed at the sight of this mocking brocade, these curtains, this overgrown room weighed down with the folds and turnbacks of its fabrics. When the shutters are closed and it's properly dark in here, I imagine a cave by the sea, a pirates' hideaway with heavy sea chests, a dramatic four-poster beside a carpet of dried seaweed, tapestries of chivalric scenes hanging from stalactites in the rock—and that rich sea smell from the silvery panels of the cave entrance, the cool, fine sand of starfish.

As we walked over to the tennis court this morning I caught a curious snippet of conversation between Jacques and Christel.

"I left *him* after our swim."

"*I* hardly saw *him* yesterday. The night before I danced with *him* at the casino … "

... and other words whose seeming triviality was transformed for me because of what I already knew for a fact (maybe I'd been listening more closely than I first thought) and because they didn't mention Allan by name. Taken like that, with the suspicious intonation that both of them were all too clearly afraid to stress, this *him* used so implicitly, so inevitably, suddenly seemed to be raised to an almost mythical level, attaining in a way just short of sacrilegious the dignity of that Large letter that takes care not to define the great, suspicious, ill-definable prowler too closely, if necessary being as ambivalent as Lucifer, the angel himself.

Am I mistaken in seeing above all in Allan (accustomed as I am, in a probably too-arbitrary way, to personalizing ideas and idealizing personalities) a *temptation*, a test—the rallying cry among our little group for anyone who has a tendency to fall apart, destroy themselves, to tear a way through the system of rare, reasonable chances that life allows us in a brief outburst as violent as a sudden rage. Or is it simply that I'm still more hostage to certain expressions in Gregory's letter than I'd have myself believe? With the way that letter has of constantly watching me from the corner of its eye—the letter that has me under its spell.

Sometimes, prompted by my taste for humorously trans-posing things, which is never quite free of an excusable note of pedantry, I christen Henri and Christel the

125

Progress Party, Irène the *Resistance Party*. And Allan is *les Trois Glorieuses*.[2]

Casimir Périer to Odilon Barrot: '*This country's misfortune is that there are people like you who think there was a revolution. No, Monsieur, there was no revolution; there was simply a change of sovereign.*'

Keyword, profound word, word somehow admirable— word that makes the opponent *close his mouth* forever. Word that belongs to a breed. The professional deniers of scandal. Those for whom there's *never* a revolution.

Those who can sense an event's dark ring, its halo, its ever-conspicuous opportunity to take flight, its whisper of a coming storm—that eternal breed of Thomases for whom stigmata will only ever be a chance to suggest applying a compress.

Once again I see the plains of Hoyerswerda. Beyond the double barbed wire of the prisoner-of-war camp the mournful Lausitz plain receded into the distance. Devoid of humanity, deserted. Every day at midday a feeble little train, tiny as a toy, scored an oblique line across the landscape. All around us, inaccessible yet on offer, stretched that wonderful promised land. Early each morning I went and gazed at a mysterious bend in the road, deep in a pinewood, a road whose poignant twists and turns would never open up for me. On frosty days when the ground rang out dully, the sun on the snow seemed to melt the bars of our cage, and great gusts of air flooded in from all round the horizon. On a variegated ocean of wooded pasture, the type that inexplicably solemnizes that English word which I can never hear without emotion—'woodland'—half-hidden behind an outcrop of copse, stretched across the eastern horizon was Hoyerswerda, the mysterious Town, the forbidden Town, gathered round a church tower that shone like brass. The superb Lausitz skies adorned it alone, magnificent great dense clouds that the sea can't catch in its quick, misty grey nets—the silkiest, fluffiest cotton wool with a hint of a storm as fine, as soft as an animal's belly—a great procession of fleets heading for the afternoon crossing. Towards them, mysteriously, fled the furrows of the potato fields—from another corner of the camp you were sometimes surprised to see it rise like a mirage over the gentle, quivering haze of a birch copse. Always on the horizon, sovereign and still, summoning up streams of desire, a fertile source for an imagination weaned on gardens, beautiful water butts, dark doorways, on sleepy well-to-do houses in the country—and for some reason at twilight on stormy evenings the magic of Northern towns rose above it from behind an angry sky: cavernous warehouses smelling of tallow and tar, their gables standing up spasmodically above a pool of heavy water, a leaden lapping noise—in an amphitheatre of lights twinkling in the mist over the bend in a river, the cross struts of great black and sooty steel bridges, that shake like beasts as the heavy express trains rumble across them: Stettin, Newcastle, Glasgow—a red-hot abyss of blast furnaces cut across by layers of cold night fog; above a ribbon of dirty pewter-coloured water, humble in its pit, gigantic landing stages, scaffolding where freight wagons plunge, like those long-legged bridges in the Rockies or the bewildering landscape of an oilfield—the transparent blackness of the air where, no sooner the clamour stops and the arpeggios of green, blue, red lights cease their clattering, a great salty blanket peppered with coal dust invades your nostrils.

I never saw Hoyerswerda—passed through on my return journey—in dismal drizzle at four in the morning. How unworthy it probably was of the boundless trust I placed in it—yet, lingering as a perfume, exasperating as an unbreached stronghold, behind its hoarse syllables trails the taste of a woman you've never had, who you'll never have.

But what does this incongruous memory want from me? These abrupt images, startling scenes from my life which for the past few days have *come back* to me more frequently like a film being developed, like a drowning man's life is said to flash before him. Yes, my whole life, dry images, obscure tarot cards, a light bundle, a strange fan of barely-discernable vignettes that I shuffle till I'm totally discouraged, as if folding and packing my scant baggage the night before a mysterious sea journey.

8th August

D REAMT LAST NIGHT—a waking dream, faint but coherent, still clear in my mind, and which despite an uncertain and even agonizing outcome leaves me with a kind of satisfaction, warmth.

I'm at the Opera with Christel and Allan. Our seats look to be the best in the house, yet judging from the yawning chasm below us they seem to be up in the gods. Especially as you get to them along enormous corridors the size of a government minister's room, at the end of which stands the usherette like a bailiff, watching constantly as we make our way across a gleaming wilderness.

They're doing *Faust* (yesterday I had my usual memories of this opera) and I don't know why but the secondary character Valentin, recognizable by a silly *imperial* and a long, elaborate and pretentious duelling sword, looms far too large in every scene, so much so that—like a braggart in a comedy—he reduces the rest of the cast to mere walk-on parts. Inevitably this can't go on without consequences for his voice: by the end of the first act he's getting hoarse, and in the middle of an odd scene which I notice takes place below the orchestra, he apologizes to the audience. A slight commotion, after which it appears that, despite being tired, the tenor who played *Lohengrin* in the matinée is going to stand in for the rest of the performance. Before going out for the interval I think to myself that tired as he might be, his good grace might earn him a sympathetic reception.

We'd barely taken our seats again when, feeling a slight draught round my shoulders I get the unpleasant suspicion that I've left not only my overcoat in the cloakroom but my tailcoat too. Yes, quite inexplicably I'm in shirtsleeves. Somewhat embarrassed I go back to the cloakroom where I soon put things right. It's on the way back that things go wrong. Put off by all the anterooms, now deserted, whose closed doors and lonely resonance with music murmuring in the background are confusing, I pick the wrong door. Suddenly the theatre seems to take on vast proportions. Increasingly alarmed I trail across steppes of red carpet, occasionally passing unexpectedly in front of a row of the audience whose disapproving "shush!" disconcerts me. The reception I predicted for the tenor is already enthusiastic: everywhere there's reverent silence. The labyrinth gets larger, leads me astray; sometimes double doors eject me into the street, sometimes, like a drowning man catches sight of land before he goes under again, the moment I feel lost I unexpectedly pass back through part of the theatre with its fervent ocean rumblings. My despair grows: it looks like I'm going to miss this act. The theatre is now open to the sky, grown to the size of a stadium, or to be more precise it looks like the horseman's view of the Fête de la Fédération[3] with its rows of banners, from my childhood history books. One last time I go through a corner of paradise lost, right up in the back row: from there you can only hear the music; and in any case a fold in the ground hides the stage. People's faces are full of unbelievable fervour. The last row doesn't end at a wall but at a row of soldiers, just their heads showing above ground, fierce eyes under the helmets—probably shouldering arms because beside each head glints the upright flash of a bayonet. Then it's the street again: devoid of courage I pace up and down the blocks of houses, more and more disoriented, lost— behind me the roof of the Opera House sometimes soars up mockingly again above a tall, nocturnal façade. What's the use? All of a sudden, in the middle of the empty street, for some reason one of those shafts surrounded by scaffolding which are a sign of council building work convinces me *once and for all* of the failure of my hopeless nocturnal wanderings.

Why am I recording this dream here? It annoys me like some laughable, scathing remark about the more dignified role I imagine myself playing. Perhaps the dream's sole purpose is to *make up for* the inner dialogue—that never-ending Hugoesque dialogue between the clown and the prince—at those times when we take ourselves too constantly, too stupidly seriously. I've always dreamt far more—and more disagreeably—at times of my life ruled by a too long-lasting and oppressive *master.*

dreams as self criticism.

9th August

C OMING BACK to the hotel alone this morning after a swim I run into the elusive owner. We have a sort of friendship. I know him of old, from a hotel in the mountains where I used to spend my holidays. He was starting out as a simple bellboy there and, I think, he's grateful for my not taking advantage of this embarrassing coincidence now he's struck it rich. Having learnt over forty years that he can trust my discretion he's become candid and direct with me, likeable.

I catch him with his forehead resting on the hall window that looks out over the sea. As I appear an old reflex from his days of 'impeccable service' makes him straighten up, and we smile hastily, vaguely feeling it's best not to go into this gesture too much.

We chat briefly about the season, which promises to be good, and then a name is soon burning my tongue (what?—even with him!) and I make a passing reference to the 'rich foreign guests' that he's fortunate enough to have staying in his hotel (I notice crossly that I instinctively hide the fact that I'm on friendly terms with Allan).

Again a slight tensing of the eyelids, a sudden wave of interest spreading across otherwise neutral waters.

"Are you perhaps talking about Monsieur Allan Murchison?"

That name with the pungent, compelling taste—I saw it form on lips that I won't be able to forget now.

"For instance."

"But he's not foreign. He's French."

"He seems rather eccentric."

"H'm!"

At this point there's a flawless adjustment in his voice, which expresses one's favourable opinion of the guest, naturally—and the no-less favourable one you have of your own judgement—the confidence that when displayed by a hotel resident such eccentricity could only be of the highest calibre—and finally, to sum up, obvious awkwardness.

" … May I speak to you as a friend for a moment? Strictly in confidence of course, just between the two of us."

"By all means."

"This Monsieur Murchison—who I might add is a delightful guest, and generous, you can take it from me— quite frightens me."

A silence, a pause. I give a tug on the line.

"Goodness!"

(Let it come out by itself. Certainly don't push him.)

"Well. I'm failing in every duty of discretion by telling you this. But I know I can trust you. The day Monsieur Murchison arrived he gave us a substantial sum of money to put in the hotel safe, a … very substantial sum."

"As much as that?"

'A million.'

"Good God! How bizarre! That's what banks are for."

133

"That's what I tried to tell him, tactfully. It's a rather worrying responsibility isn't it. We haven't got armour-plated vaults like the Banque de France."

"Of course, of course … and … it's that that's worrying you?"

"No … putting myself out for guests, after all that's my job. And seeing he insists on having thousand-franc notes to hand … No, what worries me—but actually I wonder why I'm telling you this."

"Tell me anyway."

"All right: in two weeks he's already spent half of it."

I'm afraid I wasn't able to put on quite the show of surprise that was called for. Yet I should have *seen it coming.*

All of a sudden I felt quite angry. What business did this jumped-up waiter have checking up on what a man like Allan did with his money?

"Mind you," I said stand-offishly, "that's up to him."

Suddenly he went bright red, shamefaced like a servant caught pilfering. And it was my turn to feel ashamed. Because I sensed, I *knew* his suspicions weren't base, they couldn't be.

" … But yes you're right, it is pretty odd all the same."

"Isn't it? Of course he could have taken the money out to put it somewhere else—one could imagine all sorts of things. Although the odd thing is that he's drawn it out on several occasions, as if to spend it bit by bit … "

(He knows he gambles, that's for certain! He's got his spies. The staff. He won't go so far as to tell me. And it's not up to me to get him to admit it. So let's call a halt to this.)

"Well, my dear chap ... you've got a millionaire staying who wants to have a good time, that's all."

From his somewhat apologetic smile I could tell that perhaps we didn't share the same concept of worldly happiness. But what he said next, almost inadvertently, as if mumbling to himself, made me go pale.

"A millionaire, undoubtedly. Yes, he had a million. But something tells me—I can't prove this, and maybe it's stupid—that it's everything, if you see what I mean, yes, its actually everything he's got."

"Is that it, my dear Kersaint? Are you blessed with second sight?"

"You're making fun of me, obviously. It's all too tempting for a hotel manager to play the private eye. Nonetheless there are still strange things."

"Like what?"

"He's been here a fortnight now. Well—and you can take it from me because I handle all the mail for the hotel every day—he hasn't had a single letter. Which is fairly odd for someone so ... stylish, so ... in the thick of things."

"Maybe he just wants a quiet holiday. He's cut himself off for a while."

"Yes, cut himself off ... "

Kersaint was lost in thought for a moment. He was obviously speaking with reluctance, tonelessly, taking time to choose his words—despairing of being able to use these silly clues to explain a conviction that had mysteriously, instinctively developed in the absence of any real proof. A ruffling of feathers that had *put him on*

135

his guard—and which like most ordinary people he didn't have the vocabulary to express. And it was precisely this absurd conviction, this echo of my own uneasiness, which frightened me.

" … That magnificent car he came in … it's not his. It belongs to that woman … the woman who left almost immediately."

I felt myself blush slightly.

"For goodness sake, Kersaint, anyone would think you take him for an international swindler—or I don't know, a financier on the run. You know full well he's a friend of Monsieur Gregory's."

He gave a most candid smile.

"That's not the sort of thing I had in mind."

"What then?"

He suddenly looked up.

"Then nothing. He's a peculiar man, that's all. Now you'll have to excuse me—I'm being silly. And I'm going to have to leave you. The big week is about to begin … and all this is just between the two of us, naturally … "

And he left me with the classic finger on his lips of the confidant from a comedy. What an odd Iago! I feel a sort of hatred for him now, like when you catch a voyeur unawares, suddenly amazed that you've been looking *too*. With that revoltingly acute sense of smell that the coarsest species have, he'd sniffed something out. I feel ashamed of myself, quite *deflowered*. I can almost feel the mark of a dirty hand on me, on both of us. Outrageous. As if the chief of police just collared a tragic hero.

10th August

THE DAYS DRAG BY, sleepy, unchanging. Lazy desire to stay on the bed, sprawled on the warm wool, watching the smoke rise from a cigarette—to stay here for hours, days. The midday sun crushes the beach. In the corridors, in the rooms that face the blinding sea, striped awnings cast a sickly half-light like exotic undergrowth—a day of insomnia when white bathrobes glide around.

I stayed at my window for a long time last night, watching the secretive moon rise over the sea. Caught in an amorous encounter like that beneath the great ladder of light, covered in smooth, black blisters and so very silent, it looked almost shameless, strange, full of omens like a woman's malaise.

I'm getting as anxious as a child.

11th August

ALL THOSE LIKE ME, who know that innocence and guilt are given to us at birth.

In writing this I refer almost openly to my conversation the day before yesterday.

I've been struck for a long time by the fact that passion isn't an obsession, a tight, narrow ring imposed on our anxieties, the channelling of life according to that single downward slope we're fond of describing, but more of an energetic bubbling, life in anarchy, like a body in a bath of acid. The result of this in my opinion, in the opinion of anyone who looks at it closely, is that it only achieves its full force within a group. If not it doesn't reach a state of trance, transfiguration. I don't see any passion on a desert island. But the moment there was a *theatre*, if passion hadn't existed then it would have had to be invented.

Infectious passion. Passion, child of the masses—or at least the group. I've always imagined there being a halo that immediately gives individuals who enter the magic circle all their *bite*. And in a vague sort of way it's also the idea that the man in the street has of himself. In popular novels don't they talk about whirlwinds, storms, tornados of passion? As a figure of speech it makes sense.

A tornado is something that turns a piece of straw, a 'thinking reed' if you like, into a projectile. And at the heart of the whirlwind, the all-pervading suction of that point, it's that same extraordinary speed that produces astonishing stillness.

He moves—travels—within the credibility woven by his voice, gestures, his way of walking—in a realm of plausibility, decorum, of 'respectability'. His worst peculiarities can't change that. How could you *really* say stupid things while sitting that way, standing there with that regal bearing, how could anyone be suspicious of words that come from behind the barrier of lips so scrupulous, ample, so confident?

What moves me most of all in the story of Christ is the short period between the Resurrection and the Ascension, surprising with all its mysteries, those uncertain fleeting appearances, twilit, so irrevocably the *last ones*, so heartbreaking with their air of departure—and that incredible sense of nonchalance, the *last chance*, a last-minute whim, divine insouciance. It's *him* and it isn't him—suddenly it's a face that hides for a split second, which *blazes* behind another; the feverish victory cry of a ghost, cut off from eternal rest by such idyllic, limitless affection, like a conversation by a well one evening—a traveller clad in twilight who asks a servant at an inn for something to eat—a quiet dinner under the arbour with pilgrims from Emmaus, with the light behind him—the hand that breaks the bread carelessly, taking its time: the evening is so mild, everything is just *as usual*—then at last they saw him, or what's called *seeing*, some distance away. And those suddenly dazzling words that shatter the perpetual twilight, the peace of fields after the harvest where a solemn hand rises, where a pale footprint glides, in the fear that rises from the depths of time: *'Abide with us: for it is toward evening'*, and the final words, the most savagely beautiful to come from the lips of man: *'Touch me not'*. An insane mystery, the exhilarating mood of a meteor-hunt fills a whole vast region. You imagine legionnaires on night patrol, volunteers scouring the countryside round villages—mothers on doorsteps calling their children as night falls. Wells, an unexpected source of light at dusk, which people watch over, think twice about stirring up, mirrors that are covered up—the faint light of dawn that suddenly appears at the end of a tunnel of oak trees, the invisible footprint that makes the ground tremble, burst into bloom for forty leagues around. And that rebellion, the blind hatred of the well-established, the well-protected, those who *ensconce themselves*, a taste for the ruthless manhunt which appears among close-knit families. But a small band of brothers, drunk with thirst, roam the woods and fields day and night like Maenads, drunk with unquenchable thirst, stand talking at midnight crossroads, their paths, trails, routes intersecting, because from this boldness that reveals itself, that no longer *holds back*, from this unconcealed temptation, this unremitting hammering out of the marvel, they now know beyond all possible doubt that he *will* leave.

14th August

ANOTHER PECULIAR EPISODE.
These last few days the heat has become unbearable, and after lunch, the hotel now empty, I'd taken refuge in the smoking room with Jacques where for want of anything better we played a few games of chess—which he lost, not without the odd fit of temper. As the days go by I also sense him becoming more nervous too, more unstable. Once again Allan had slipped away with Christel after lunch, and Jacques, who was secretly watching them, became sullen.

He probably saw these suspicions in my eyes, and I think it was out of bravado (he's very young), to prove to me that it wasn't a woman's place to interfere with his friendship with Allan, that he suddenly offered to show me an ivory chess set, a museum piece that Allan had apparently brought back from India.

"But Allan's just gone out."

"We can go in anyway. I get on well enough with him for him not to take offence."

At that quiet time of afternoon the long corridors were empty. On the floor where Allan was staying the sun, already quite low, made lush flowery patches, stately, sleepy rosettes on the red carpet with its pattern of leaves. After the echoing staircase the sound of suddenly muffled

141

footsteps heading for his room made our intrusion seem somehow suspect. A vague recollection of the story Allan told that night, of my dream, came back to me. More than anything the red carpet seemed astonishing.

As we went in I felt so uneasy that I almost held Jacques back by the arm. I know the outward camaraderie that I suspect exists between him and Allan is the kind that permits anything and everything—which makes you immune. Of course there's nothing to worry about with him. But how could I make Jacques realize that this blank cheque didn't cover me. If Allan suddenly came back and caught us in his room he'd give Jacques a slap on the back—and I'd feel myself blush.

When it's a real piece of clothing made of stone, a shell moulded, pulled out of shape by everyday wear, how intrigued, how misled I am—much more so than by deserted houses—by a room someone has just left, still warm like a discarded coat, and where a few scattered sheets of paper, underwear, a sense of some frantic expectation, an act postponed, are, more than any other evidence, enough to make it more uniquely authentic than a face. Yes, in a way I still believe in the revelatory power of the *darkroom*.

I once wrote a moral tale. Damocles is banqueting with friends. They laugh, drink hard, call for the dancers and flute-players. The party get up from the table the worse for wine, and as the last one leaves he briefly opens the door to the empty room again, remembering he's left his crown behind. Suddenly *rooted* to the spot, for the first time he sees the sword hanging from its cord above the empty throne.

The motionless patches of sunlight on the leaf-patterned plush, the lush pools of rich yellow light on the fabric panelling, on the old-fashioned velvet armchairs left in the corridor (they're moving the furniture from one of the rooms), this yawning silence suddenly conjures up a sleepy old hotel down a leafy street in a provincial town where a grandmother, bonneted and bodiced in starched lingerie, wanders from room to room like a silent apparition, listening to the sound of the latticework of the trees, bent over by a solemn wind, moving on the velvet-shadowed walls outside the window, to the regular creaking of the furniture in the scorching afternoon.

Coming from the half-darkness of the corridor Allan's door opened onto an ocean of blazing light, and as we went in a stiff breeze made the curtains flap wildly. Ahead of us a window wide open on the splendour of the sun-drenched sea, on rough murmurings, the snapping of the breeze, made me think of escapes, rope ladders, immediately summoning up the familiar image of the *empty cage*, whose secret humour inspires the greatest dreams of levitation.

To the right of the door another window looked out over the trees in the grounds. A magnificent stairway of blustery green treetops—yellow-green, grey-green, bronze-green—climbed by stages towards the sharp, openwork tip of a larch high in the sky.

While Jacques bustled about like the regular visitor he was, rummaging through drawers and cupboards without the slightest embarrassment, I looked round with unprepared eyes, that innocent privilege of the first glance, so quick to uncover things, which would never be mine again. Yet in a room that at first seemed laid waste by a brutal, almost blinding stream of brightness, thanks to the green half-light from the right, from the nimble darkness of the trees, the hiding places, the shadiest corners were able to set up their defence, protect their threatened privacy, their shorter and more remarkable lifespan, their more persistent memories.

The moment the door opened I'd got the impression of an unusually *vast* room, yet thinking back there was nothing about its dimensions, admittedly imposing although not excessive, which seems to bear that out. It was more a particular play of light that swept the whole length of the room, the unaccountable way certain pieces of furniture were placed, empty clearings above a suddenly bare stretch of carpet that made the room seem inexplicably *airy*, recreating the intoxicating pleasure that only the simple act of breathing mountain air can produce. To my mind such impressions are only linked with the heights of luxury and elegance, an instinctive, discovered elegance that you don't find in current furnishing styles, always prone to follow trends, to shabbily *use* space by imitating the layout of pillboxes and battleships.

Yet at the same time it dawned on me that the lack of originality common to all hotel rooms was absent from this one. By the window looking onto the trees the furnishings had a more personal feel, revealed at least superficially by the few assorted trinkets, the object of some secret passion which the colonist, the sailor, the explorer tucks away in his trunk when needs be, then by the light of the desert stars tries to give them back their own particular, obsessive familiarity. A coat of thick royal blue wool hung lengthways on the wall, a heavy priestly style, unusual, which I don't know why but I straightway imagined being a souvenir of Allan's trip to the Himalayas. Further along an old cricket bat and cap, some valuable Indian weapons, a heavy chest made of black wood and studded all over with nails and brass stars, Arab workmanship of unusual richness. Rudderless, anxious as blind men in the painful daylight of the room, huddled beside a long low leather couch as if to keep warm, these objects conjured up the folds of an invisible tent around them, recreated that minimal, removable decor, patiently enhanced by familiar ghosts, which is all the opium addict needs to conceal the horrors of changing scenery from himself while on his travels.

Also on the wall were polished metal plaques of arabesque figures, worryingly intertwined, which play a minor role in Tibetan magic and which vaguely reminded me of the cave paintings in the adventures of Arthur Gordon Pym. An evening coat, scarf and white tie were heaped on an armchair. The icy atmosphere, increased by this shivery little alcove moored alongside the room like a lifeboat, the streams of light that delved into the corners, reflected off the smooth surfaces, reminded me of some kind of *high place*, a last refuge, the dome of an observatory, the roof terrace of a skyscraper, the *watchtower* at the top of a lighthouse, the upper floor of a tall building where the hunted fugitive suddenly gives in to the irresistible call of the void that surrounds him, offering itself …

Meanwhile Jacques was chattering, flitting round the room, producing rare trinkets from drawers, a Chinese fan, a piece of cashmere, a magnificent midnight blue shawl dotted with stars, apparently not suffering from the uneasiness that fixed me to the spot, dragged out my movements and silences—a paralyzing self-consciousness, the constant contradictions that made the wooden floor pitch and reel on the swell.

Yes, I'm ill! ... ill.

While looking for somewhere to put the chessboard that Jacques had finally found in a drawer I saw a small card table by the door. In full view on the green baize lay an unopened letter—probably put there by the staff after the afternoon post. I remembered the manager's awkward remarks and stared at the square of paper with particular interest. It was addressed in female handwriting, long, elegant, imperious. What strange urgency could it bear witness to, this letter that had fallen into the depths of the void, the silence of this room? Dolorés? The envelope suddenly fascinated me, embodying as it did the agonizing feelings with which the room had overwhelmed me since we came in. To clear a space for Jacques I picked it up off the table—it burnt my fingers, and in my hurry to get rid of it clumsily put it on the bed.

A strange fear now took shape in me. The fear that Allan would come back and discover us—discover *me*—in his room. Dazed, numb, more and more paralyzed I watched Jacques talk, come and go, act incomprehensibly. Could it be possible that he didn't realize we *had* to leave? The thought that we were going to be discovered, discovered here, became more unbearable with every second—yet without me feeling able to make the slightest movement, say the slightest word to get Jacques to leave. Quite the opposite; with a fixed mechanical smile I encouraged him to keep talking, to circle round me, numb me with his beehive buzzing, his frantic bustling. Suddenly it was the savagery of those nightmares where you're being chased, where the killer gets closer, closer—and it would be enough to press this switch, call out, open that door—but the hand I raised fell back again, lifeless, paralyzed, the words stuck in my throat. Now he would definitely come—he's back at the hotel, he's coming up the stairs.

Footsteps echoed at the far end of the corridor. With incredible detailed clarity I distinctly heard Allan say goodbye to Christel outside her door—and at the same time I noticed Jacques looking at me open-mouthed—and, still smiling mechanically, I realized I hadn't answered a question that Jacques must have asked a few moments before. Nerves at breaking point I heard the footsteps get closer, the door open. At last! With my whole being I felt that same sense of release that a criminal must have after he's confessed.

I admit all this is barely believable—barely defensible.

Allan stopped in the doorway and stared at me for a split second, quite taken aback—then that wonderful ease of his reasserted itself and he showed me round his residence in the least affected, most delightful way ... reddening, paling—first talking effusively, volubly, then struck helplessly dumb like a pendulum gradually returns to its point of equilibrium—I was finally about to pull myself together when from the corner of my eye I caught sight of the *letter*, and suddenly I felt lost—sensed I was about to lose it.

For a moment the conversation went in fits and starts—that's to say I made insane efforts, heart pounding, head spinning giddily, to come out with a few words. Somewhat surprised at my discomfiture, every now and then Allan gave me an odd sideways glance. I was extraordinarily agitated.

"There's a letter on the bed for you," I managed to say, throat obviously tightening. I felt beads of sweat breaking out on my face and hands. I couldn't have spoken at a worse moment, right in the middle of Allan talking, like someone who rushes in breathlessly to say there's a fire or that someone has just died.

This time there was something so shocking about what I'd said that even Jacques, whose innocence throughout the whole scene seemed so complete as to be scarcely believable, glanced up sharply and stared at me stupidly. Another moment went by in appalling embarrassment.

Then, frowning slightly now, Allan went and got the letter without saying a word or taking his eyes off me.

Reading back over this I smile bitterly at the lengths to which an imagination that claims to be under control is capable of going. How do I account for this almost unbelievable feebleness, so unjustified—a total loss of nerve when confronted by childish fears? The memory of that absurd anxiety still brings me out in a cold sweat—my jaw clenches involuntarily. Am I going mad?

15th August

IN MY CONFUSION I'm still trying to understand what it was about that room that could have caused the mournful impression I got yesterday, that panic. Nothing I can see. It's a room like any other. A totally reassuring room. The moment he came in Allan's gesture, that good-natured, welcoming, incidental gesture (he had a slight moment of hesitation), seemed to say: "There's nothing to find in here".

When you look hard, determinedly at a piece of furniture, a portrait, a detail of a carpet in isolation, choosing to be *detached* from everything else, it sometimes happens that by *seeing* them as they are, with that particular presence they'll always have, everything absolutely irreducible that eventually emerges from them for whatever possible reason, in response to whatever rational appeal—to the point of making everything else suddenly invisible—anything which implies that they *are*, anything in them which might suggest what they could also be, when suddenly you no longer feel able to say 'it's nothing but that'—then on rare occasions you sometimes feel that inescapable panic I felt yesterday.

A curious detail comes back to me now, seeming to excuse me belatedly for dropping the reins for a second, for abandoning that room to wander shamefully in time. On Allan's desk a calendar with thin, removable ivory

149

leaves showed one date very clearly: 8th October. A silly mistake, or the invisible key to this spell—like when reading at night you suddenly sit up, puzzled, listening in the familiar bedroom which the clock that stopped ticking a moment ago has just abandoned, with the great steady humming of an express train, to some dizzying downward slope.

Why not imagine that wherever he goes Allan has one of those focal points for grievances hidden somewhere about him, which in serious cases medicine has come to see as one of the most drastic but effective ways of saving the whole body. Attracting to himself, out of compassion, all the toxins, unwelcome cells, all the deadly elements that are always scattered round even the healthiest body.

When in the final act of *Lohengrin* the hero returns dressed from head to foot in the same silver armour you saw him arrive in in the first act, you immediately realize he's about to leave—that for the second and final time this parabola, this orbiting star that follows the satellite of the Grail is going to cross the path of the earth's eclipse. The wings on his helmet are like a comet that disappears forever into the darkness of space. And if Elsa, if the king looked at him for the first time at that moment then they'd feel something of what I feel—this disintegration of the human being in the wave, the open sea, this stifling and giddy vertigo that constricts the heart.

150

I remember another moment in the opera. The middle of the bedroom scene, right in the middle of the fatal duet. With the maliciousness of an angel Elsa has just asked the first, fearsome question. The fatal spark. A mysterious hesitation still drags on the strings of the orchestra, creating a shimmer round a faint, irreparable fissure, the heart-sinking feeling of stepping over the edge. I remember how my hands trembled as we got to that part in the score often emphasized by a stage direction: '*Lohengrin kisses Elsa tenderly, and going to the window shows her the garden in full bloom*'. Out of the window is the most beautiful moonlit night, a sleepless night frightened by unusual breezes, a silent turbulence of pallid petal whorls—a night of omens when the flowers move around. The rising moon, the distant moon, disappointing, a trickster, the moon that falls short of expectations, the one that frightens Romeo:

> *O! Swear not by the moon, the inconstant moon …*
> *That tips with silver all these fruit-tree tops.*[4]

In the sky, shouldering arms, twinkle all the cruel stars of Chaldea. A night sealed by bluish, mineral light. And then the hero, in profile, one foot on a stone seat, chin in hand, leans his elbows on the casement, and in the depths of this night of shattered hopes, hopes mysteriously consummated, from the depths of a night pierced with distant enigmatic fanfares, in a false, fantastic dawn, its light battling that of the torches, in the distance he makes out the priestly soaring of a swan, the silty estuary of the

Scheldt where the nocturnal flood tide covers the beaches, the lapping of the high tide, the swell of the sea, now well-established and holding its head up like a horse— and already the bow of a mysterious ship is breaking his heart: tomorrow we'll sail the seas.

Why must I picture Allan always hesitating on this edge, bathed in this double light, always acting *in both scenes?* Sometimes when I see him, sense him so detached, so free, playing with life with such unreal indifference, I imagine confusedly that he's on the verge of a winning move of supreme importance, for unbelievable stakes—that, all thought of mundane success set aside, he's actually playing double or quits. That amazing ease, that abandon in his smile, to find its like you'd have to imagine a tightrope walker who, in a blaze of light with a dark chasm either side, moves forward on the taut high wire and reveals, by the lack of any stage direction, the nerve-wracking wonder of what it can be to suddenly walk straight ahead.

With him everything is destined for disaster, everything is condemned. He takes the colour out of everything. It's impossible not to see that he's thrown down an insufferable challenge. At Roscaër he amused himself by walking along the edge of the void on the top of the wall. It wasn't simply a childish prank. What's more, it's this childish behaviour, which naturally he wouldn't stoop to so much as explain, which to me perhaps best reveals the brutally provocative nature, that *inexpiable* nature he can't help but give to the most trivial actions.

The preservation of life no doubt basically stems from an enormously patient, hesitant effort, something everyone pushes themselves to do, keeping an eye on themselves on the difficult path of perseverance. Life probably couldn't continue without a painstakingly-maintained worldwide conspiracy. It seems that having Allan nearby continually encourages me to make those ill-considered little gestures that distinguish life from death, the rational from the immeasurable—which with a second's loss of self-control would lead to ruin. In a railway carriage, opening the door onto the line *instead*; pointing a revolver in such-and-such a direction just *to see*; signing a cheque—why not?—which will definitely *bounce*; gestures whose imminence, kept constantly at a distance from us at the cost of such unremitting tension that eventually, like the acrobat on his high wire we cease to be conscious of it, make me think of something I read by some philosopher: '*The devil is in the unexpected*'.

I must set aside certain preliminaries, isolate the invisible, get to *the heart of the matter*.

A certain talent for lavish, volatile evaporation, like the dazzling shower of a waterfall inside its rainbow, is the distinctive feature of those haunting individuals through whom the world so easily takes on for us the colours they steal from it.

Irène can't stand him. She wearies me with her bitter-sweet remarks, the incessant allusions. "The *homme fatal*, the common or garden buck, the fashionable dancer."

She tries to convince me that it would be humiliating for Christel to fall in love like a schoolgirl for a film star.

She doesn't know, she doesn't sense, that a certain cut and dried style, the severe, ruthless stamp—definitely *take it or leave it*—of a finely chiselled profile, that slightly coarse, glaring distinctiveness that subdues and stupefies the masses, only scares off the semi-refined and creates empathy between the simple-hearted crowd and those for whom it isn't just sheer naivety to demand that they should be *marked out* by this irrefutable sign—this image of a prodigy that we are inexplicably starved of by all the violent figures in history, and in whose face something more obscure than human reason invariably falters and capitulates—people we're forever destined to judge by a quite different standard than that of good taste.

18th August

NOW I KNOW why I was so struck by Gregory's letter, kept in a state of alarm, as if warned. That letter which didn't require a reply was precisely the sort that initiates a correspondence—but is no doubt also as necessary and extraneous to it as the siphon that feeds a series of communicating vessels.[5] Certain letters, written in a certain tone, are sure to pave the way for others. Except the correspondents aren't guaranteed to stay the same. Quite the reverse. It's more a matter of signals which, suddenly crossing your path in the dark like a pencil of light feeling its way from a lighthouse, seem designed to bring you up to date on your position, warn you that you're approaching dangerous waters. For these messages from inspired blind men, at times of particularly sharp, palpable tension the word correspondence itself is suddenly sublimated and the Baudelairean meaning simply reasserts itself. At one point in my life I was bombarded with anonymous letters—which I managed to convince myself, despite all the possible methods of concealment, admittedly weren't in the same ink or handwriting. But then at a time of deep moral depression I was no doubt just the injured chicken who attracts pecks from a distance. Perhaps it's a flight path, a tangle of radio waves of which I'm not aware and with which I must have got crossed, like you accidentally overhear a telephone conversation, two phone calls with no obvious destination—genuine monologues which, if put in some chance envelope would rely on luck, go the wrong way, get lost, those courses of action hard to explain to a stranger. I was talking about anonymous letters. There aren't just unsigned letters; there are also unaddressed letters. Perhaps the only letters I want to receive now are those where I feel conscience-bound to read the address twice.

There's a strange ambiguity in that banal, everyday expression, *the man of the moment*. The one the tangle of circumstances just happens to put at the centre of a situation whose consequences essentially make him an outsider to it—the one whose hand also holds that small weight, the faint impetus that will completely tip the scales.

This morning I got a letter from Christel. Just why—being able to speak to me so easily—did she choose the more formal, appealing form of communication that is writing? But the best thing is to reproduce the letter—

My friend,
Don't be surprised if I call you that. A friend is what you've been since that evening, or rather that night we spent together on the dunes. I've known since that night that I can count on you. If I've seemed distant since then, preoccupied, I beg you not to hold it against me. I'm unhappy. I need to tell you that, and I need your advice.

Since that day at Kérantec you've known, haven't you? I've no hope at all. I've had no hope from the start. There's that woman.

And above all I realized immediately that Allan isn't someone you can get. You can't reach him. Among so many well-established people, as easy-going and non-existent as the furniture, he moves, he's already en route, in his eyes there's the look of the traveller at the door of the train as it gradually pulls away—the way he looks people up and down, quickly, distractedly, even those he likes, then promptly fixes his gaze straight ahead. And that same hurried awkwardness, the same last-minute what's the point *of some tragic rendezvous on a station platform. How could anyone think of living with him? I can feel the minutes slipping hopelessly past. I'm sad, so terribly sad.*

Allan's behaviour toward me is such that I don't know where I stand. I don't know whether it's utmost kindness or utmost deceitfulness (kindness or deceit being things that couldn't be said to sap the character of a man like Allan). In his better moments I get that same attentive, considerate gentleness that the seriously ill show for people who sit at their bedside: in the other person they're caressing the reflection of their own ordeal.

Yes, he likes being with me, walking alone with me. Sometimes he takes me off for long walks. He talks to me in the gentlest way possible. He takes my hands in his and looks at me. At those moments I'd give anything to be a comfort to him—he seems so sad. Everyone here hates him, what I mean is that nobody understands him, they don't like him as he deserves to be liked. Except you, I know it, I'm sure of it. And forgive me for saying so, I'm your friend for that too. After all, perhaps he makes them uneasy.

I can feel time running through my fingers like sand. Sometimes I look at the sea and the dunes, the pines, the beach huddled at the end of the bay, and it's as if I can feel this landscape deep inside me like an apparition that suddenly melts away, dissolves.

I'm like a traveller who stops off briefly at an unknown island, breathes the divinely gentle air that for him won't have time to lose its freshness, and for whom for a moment at least the earth is gentle too. And it's true that Allan is close to me in the same way as a long journey is close.

My mother's amazed I'm staying here so long. My holidays always tended to be more movable. Yes, it's true I've changed. Here I'm not thinking of anything more than a wonderful journey through the months, the weeks. I'll see the sun grow pale and the nights turn cool, empty hotels, shivery October mornings over a sparkling sea. I'll hear the wind in woods full of stillness, behind the unseeing houses, suddenly so stunted, so intimidated, that great loud noise of the wind, and I'll walk alone on the pine needles in the slanting light of empty autumn days. Eyes closed I'll feel myself sink into this little town, evacuated like one of those towns in the American desert after the mine closes down. Empty gardens behind rusty railings will open up for me, their secret late autumn flowers dusted with sea bitterness by the freely blowing wind. I'll hear the last doors slam, keys turning in the last locks. Then there'll be the first morning frosts, a fire in the uncomfortable villa, startled woodwork that yawns and creaks; cold draughts slipping in through bigger gaps under the doors. A gaping drawn-out afternoon with a numbed cockerel that crows in a last yellow ray of light. Then one morning I'll wake up in another world, beside a beach covered in snow that the rising tide eats into with the sound of a branding iron plunged into water, the red-hot iron disc of sun from a winter's tale above a magnificent length of ermine, the biting gentleness of a sunny afternoon in the empty streets. I'll be alone here with Allan.

Sometimes he can be very detached, bitter, very offensive—so concerned with proving that he's playing with me, that of course nothing could happen. Sometimes he takes me into that little wood that's always green which stretches behind the chapel, a faint mist of hazel and willow beyond wonderful dark green lawns. We lie on the grass and soon find we've nothing more to say to each other—just stare at the sky, watch luminous patches moving between the branches. Time doesn't go by for us there like elsewhere, but freezes—like in those sacred groves in allegorical paintings where the airy movements of a young girl suddenly stop forever and she becomes a figure in Botticelli's Primavera, in that moonlike undergrowth at the height of day, all those swags of creeper wreathed round the branches and, as if caught by frost in this vivid chiaroscuro like in a window, so many sleeping beauties. Ah! I wish some magic power would send me to sleep with him forever, make me die to this world of ghosts and, lying side by side in the funeral barge, finally dead to the world, slip away to that foreign country from which a curse has banished him and to which everything calls him back.

And then night falls, and in the depths of the suddenly dark copse he listens closely to the clocks striking, their sounds repeated by the twilight.

Being with him you quickly lose your attachment to anything, like old people when they're close to death. For the gentleness that's in him, the secretive, friendly complicity to finally give unstintingly of itself, you'd need to imagine the beloved eyelids that a hand closes in death, that rough yet friendly gesture, the mild authority of female fingers laying out the body, the hands they fold on the sheet with a mysterious smile. Yes, I'd like Allan to be there when I die. Apart from that perhaps he has nothing to say to me. But I'd *like that. He'd simply take this hand that belongs to him, and I'd let him lead me. There'd be no more words, just trust.*

But I realize I'm way off the subject of my letter. So now I summon my strength to ask the question on which everything depends for me—my last chance. You probably don't know him well. But he has an exceptionally high regard for you. I don't think there's anyone here who's capable of understanding, of fathoming out this impenetrable person like you can.

Who is Allan?

What I expect in reply, you realize, isn't a portrait, an analysis. I think—and maybe this is insane, maybe it's mad, but I have this requirement—you must be able to reply to every question with a single word. One question about him—you're the only one who understands this—can only be answered by an oracle. There's a finger on him, a light around him that makes everything else fade. I want to know what it is that's making signs to me through him.

Christel

19th August

CHRISTEL'S LETTER made me aware of my laziness, my inherent cowardice. Today I rub my eyes and wake up to that determined voice. I can't just keep on musing over this disconcerting character indefinitely. I'm going to have to reply—and it's not just Christel, it's Allan, Allan most of all who requires a reply. Either that or I'll have to run away like Gregory.

I stayed. Whatever I do now I'm committed—to what? I still don't know. There are people who refuse to put up with impartial witnesses, drive away the bystander, force him to take sides, beat the war drums as loudly as they can, the fanatical partisan. Allan came here to bring a sword. This letter proves it.

22nd August

READ CHATEAUBRIAND'S *La vie de Rancé* over the last few days—no doubt driven by that divinatory instinct that always leads me unwittingly to the book that's particularly in tune with my mood. Incredible book, jotted down pell-mell, I mean sketched out with the careless, mythical claw of the *griffin*,[6] the monster with the lightning touch that's the born writer. Branchy, bristly, hunchbacked, foreboding—it's like those charred grey tree-like cinder patterns that a thunderbolt leaves behind. It has a taste of Ash Wednesday, the robust astringency of those cold, clear, exhilarating September mornings that seem to make everyone in the world suddenly move house—the footsteps of the removal men come to look over the apartment echo clearly in attics and wine cellars. Then you think you're rushing headlong through ghostly furnished rooms, dreamlike attics where sequined dresses rustle, where petticoats fly in the breeze, yellowed, matchless pieces of lace, doublets, feather bonnets—in the faint jingle of bones coupling—a frantic, ghostly farandole that reminds you of Molière's Don Juan. Now and then a pungent, world-weary phrase, tasting of a dead leaf spat out long ago in a vineyard stripped by the grape harvest, chews over the bitterness like an old horse.

You also think of Baudelaire:

162

Once the heart is harvested …

New paths mapped out by a desperado pen, new shoots already growing at the foot of the hoary old trunk wearied by moss—suddenly, in a corner of the page, Cocteau, Radiguet.

> *… Rancé had success preaching in various churches. His words poured out in streams like those of Bourdaloue would later, but he spoke more movingly and less quickly.*

> *In 1648 that ditch opened up which France leapt into in order to climb the ladder of liberty. This orgy of blood blurred the roles; woman took command; the Duke of Orléans wrote letters to:* 'their Ladyships the Countesses and Brigadiers in my daughter's army against Mazzarino'.

You think you hear stealthy footsteps walking through this book, emptied in great spadefuls like the graveyard in Hamlet—where the echoes are richer, purer, as in a series of empty rooms where you distinctly hear dry twigs cracking underfoot on the icy winter path. Something's coming: what a surprise! Is it Death? It's just death.

A book made up wholly of harmonics, like a worn-out harp that now only plays out of dulled compassion, half-frozen, muted. It's the most poignant *Nunc Dimittis* in the whole of our literature.

However complex, widespread, interconnected the vascular system might be, all the blood from every vein can still flow out through a single wound—so strong is its desire in the dark depths of its prison to at last see daylight—to *get everything out into the open.*

23rd August

NEAR THE CASINO, facing the sea, where the beach ends at a sudden bend the familiar landscape of wind-blown dunes scattered with soft, bitter, salt-grey flowers unexpectedly begins. Here a leafy road leads out from a sharp corner onto a low, bare stone wall that runs along the beach, where for long periods, sheltered from the wind, the rain leaves large dark green pools in which clouds make their escape. The wind rises like a wall all along the edge of the shifting expanse. Beside these granite verges, this long, unfamiliar, unattractive parapet that borders the sea like a kind of fortress glacis made of hard foundation stones, I've often thought of some abandoned palace, an oceanic Versailles facing the sea for all eternity, cast off on its misty overhangs—*forming one body* with the mist, the clouds, like the ponderous fading outline of a battleship.

A kind of indecisive vacuum pervades this gloomy place where you turn your back on houses that are just trying to get on with their awkward, uncertain lives. This palace I dream of would be there to hide the debris of some great disaster. Dismal rooms whose stone floors would harshly echo the sounds of the sea. A flight of huge, dramatic stone steps plummeting into the waves as far as the eye can see, baring its unassailable rocky teeth at the fickle droning of their womanly rage. Sometimes a faded beam of sunlight would create the colours of the beyond between banks of mist, that unreal glimmer above the place of limbo, the soft, glassy sash of water encircling the drowning man as, priestly and upright, he sinks down into the magnificent peace of the deep.

For want of sun you probably have to give up hope of seeing day break over these dissolving strands of mist where lighthouses are used to working at midday, seagulls' wings flapping against window in this soft, sightless glow that reflects in puddles on an empty road after rain in the early hours. Land in limbo still exhausted by the flood, a feeble revitalizing of flesh as spongy as a jellyfish, still floating like hair just below the surface in great shipments of seaweed and currents. Yet daylight seeps in, gains entry, sweeps through, engulfs the darkness with that same complex web the tide uses to fill the channels on the beach. But for a long time the landscape still hangs below the horizon, weighed down yet unburdened, absorbed by the watery mass like a ship overwhelmed by heavy seas.

It was on this wild esplanade, rippling everywhere with wave-volleys breaking in the grey morning, like the bed of a woman who rolls over, heavy and tired after the night, that I'd arranged to meet Allan.

As seven o'clock was striking I saw him in the distance, coming along the seashore, a tall, blasé, elegant silhouette—unusually lively in the pale morning. An ironic half-smile on his lips as he came up to me: in front of me, impenetrable, relaxed and taut, was the poker player set on seeing his luck through to the end.

How solemn, how stirring it is to be shut away here with him. I'm so moved by his presence. I'm confident of his goodwill. I feel a great friendly affection for him. He's so engaging. Like meeting a woman for a first date, despite myself the first words to spring to my lips would be those of great, profound gratitude: "You came!" But already he's talking, he's here, deep in that same solemn seriousness—and so now it begins.

"My dear Gérard, what's so serious that I have to come all the way out here?"

Yet his smile was slightly sad, uneasy, his nostrils twitched a little.

"Don't laugh—you'll take away what little courage I have. Because what I've got to say is serious."

"Believe me I'm aware of that, and might I say I'm flattered."

Suddenly it was all so difficult. We walked by the sea for a moment, hesitant, not speaking. This encounter in the grey morning, so slow to take shape, the unusual isolation, the slightly awkward earnestness of meeting at dawn, the dreadful chill of morning—faced with the incoherence of this enterprise my courage suddenly failed me. Absurdly, with no further ado, in full view of this calm sea I was going to order Allan to bare his soul to me. The madness of my undertaking rose up in front of me like a wall.

Yet in Allan's eyes, which saw my all-too-obvious embarrassment, I suddenly detected a brief, odd glimmer of sympathy—and I sensed help was at hand. His wonderful sense of courtesy, of *decorum* in such situations would instinctively smooth the way, at least bring about an honourable outcome from this worst of dead ends.

"Believe it or not I've been expecting this summons for several days."

I glanced at him in amazement.

"Yes. I won't make a secret of it. Since the day I found you—that's the polite word but to satisfy your vanity if you like I'll say: *caught* you in my room at the hotel. After the house search—with the best of intentions, naturally—comes the interrogation."

I'd been discovered, yes; and yet I felt a gentle, ingratiating warmth creeping through me. I'd been put *at ease*.

" … Because it was slightly more than a friendly visit. No, don't deny it—your hands are shaking. You were *had*, my dear Gérard, and I'd have had to be blind not to see through your suspicious pretence of innocence."

"So!" he added, suddenly looking down at his feet and shrugging. "Why beat about the bush. Now you know."

"What?"

With what a wild voice—enough to make me go white with shame and amazement—I let out that cry.

"What I've come here to do."

"All right Allan! Let's get to the point. I'll play fair the same as you. That's what I've come to ask you this morning."

From Allan, who I daren't look at at that precise moment—my heart was pounding—I just caught a little whistle of admiration. This slight hint of coarseness suddenly betrayed his less-than-total peace of mind.

"Oh yes, a direct attack. But my dear Gérard, allow me to point out a slight inconsistency. You've come here ready for the fray, a difficult joust. And you're no mean jouster I can tell you. Then when the right opening appears you promptly change plan, close your eyes and strike the fatal blow. But lo-and-behold, luck isn't on your side—I don't go down."

Yet even now that gentle, warm, tender note of empathy in his voice.

"What is there for you to deny if you think I've 'guessed'?"

"Guessing is simply the word I give to the most triumphant moment of the quest. The truth is depressing, you know that. It disappoints us because it restrains. It grips hard then lets go, like a hand throwing something away. It's poor, has to sell off its furniture and possessions. But at the sight of a slightly higher truth, although still only sensed, in any sensitive soul love blossoms so it can be invited in, a major adjustment that's a sign of communion with the source of nourishment it wants. It's that near-mystical asceticism, that accurate, almost miraculous premonition of affinity between desire and what it thrives on, the higher approaches that lead to the Holy Table, which I call guessing. I think that's the point you're at."

He lowered his voice, suddenly firm and serious.

"Are you asking me to now refuse to satisfy this hunger by suppressing it? Are you really sure you want to know?"

"For heaven's sake drop this mockery Allan. Put a stop to this infernal controversy you carry round with you

169

everywhere. Can't we talk seriously? I'm asking you as a friend."

"You're well aware, I think, that that friendship is reciprocated. And if I regret anything it's not being able to give you more definite proof *now* of its total lack of self-interest."

"Why make such a point about this 'now'? What's the mystery? Can't you see you're being offensive?"

"*Once and for all* do stop trying to catch me out. I thought it was agreed between us that we were above such polite hints. Or maybe we've still got a long way to go."

"What makes you think I'm following you?"

"Yes, you're following me. Since the day we talked in the smoking room you've done nothing else."

"So where are you taking me?"

"You might say that that joke rings hollow. Just try repeating it, *laughing* at the same time. But probably—at this point I'll drop a few grains of beneficial truth … "

There was suddenly a slight distance in his voice, a bitterness that made me feel I'd been cut off brutally by cold steel.

" … nowhere. That's your fate. Although I'll tell you now that later on you'll regard this moment, when you made for the open sea like an explorer lusting after discovery, as an inspired and honourable point in your life."

"Prophecies now! It beggars belief! Making grandiose predictions while hiding behind a veil of secrecy that's all too easy to pluck out of thin air doesn't impress me. People who tell me my fortune without being asked annoy me—in return I'll warn you of that."

For once I'd got rather heated. But I felt Allan suddenly slacken the line. He obviously wasn't keen for the conversation to come to an abrupt halt.

"That cut your dignity to the quick, my dear Gérard. I must say it's almost admirable. But I hope you won't mind if I'm not as offended as you seem to want me to be. Just now you thought that the fact of me suspecting, even being certain that you'd guessed, was going to bring about some kind of confession from me. So I'll draw your attention to an important shade of meaning.

"Why not indulge my taste for moral tales? Do you remember the crucial scenes in *Crime and Punishment?* There's no doubt that Porfiri knows, but—and that's the whole point—Raskolnikov doesn't confess. Admittedly there's no longer any mystery, but he's holding the last piece of evidence. As long as he keeps quiet he knows the magic circle won't close, that everything will keep on dangling in mid air, awaiting the final conclusion. Although there's nothing, not a single line that hasn't been deciphered, he still holds the key in his hand, the seal that's placed on an adventure that's finished—as long as the word isn't spoken, stays there open-mouthed on some unidentified horizon. Haven't you ever wondered about the exhilarating power of the criminal who clenches his teeth on the magic word that everyone is gasping to hear, at which everything is going to collapse? In both, profound senses of the word—confession. Seen from that point of view, in my opinion the final page, the in every way and necessarily dramatic dénouement—the crowd, the public square, the sudden solemnity—perhaps only unconsciously aims to restore, in practical terms, the sacred, conclusive, excessive character of his *confession*, that superhuman *quotation*, that light of annunciation into which humanity was created to vanish, to disappear— that faint glow of the summit over the abyss which, for humanity, distinguishes a certain truth from an *obvious* one."

"I'll have to leave empty-handed then. You won't shed any light on what you've come here to do—on the role you've given yourself to play."

"I think everything I've just said shows I've no intention of shying away from what vindicates me. But it's me who decides the time and place. Don't worry, my dear Gérard, I'll *declare* myself. When the time comes."

"I have to admit that this certainty does nothing to put my mind at rest. Quite the reverse. Swear to me you haven't come here to do something evil."

"You sound like a priest! I find these resolutions utterly objectionable. Have I really shocked you so deeply? Has my behaviour, or, to use your language, my example— because I don't acknowledge any other form of action— taken on such decisive authority for you? You have to admit you're contradicting yourself."

"Never mind the worn-out flourishes. This isn't about me. It's about Christel."

I'd burnt my bridges now. What needed to be said was going to be said, thank God.

Was I mistaken? On Allan's face, which up till now had displayed nothing but dull, kindly benevolence—an indif- ference that prevented anything dramatic from creeping into our discussion—I could just make out a suddenly sharper, more dangerous expression appearing …

Yes, his face changed! And in an instant a sudden fear shot through me. Behind those eyelids, shrouded for a moment by a slight mistiness like leucoma, a sort of terrible unseeing opaqueness, something suddenly sprang up, a glimmer of biting, fearsome concentration that told me in no uncertain terms that the real game had *now* begun.

"How does that young girl come to figure in this? I was under the impression we were talking more generally."

"It's not as strong an impression as you'd like it to be. But since it's necessary I'll spell it out for you."

Ironically Allan put on the conventional, delighted pose of the well-bred man whose companion sees, as Stendhal said, *'his chance to give a long, elegant recital'*.

But I realize here that I'll be capturing the quite distinctive atmosphere of this conversation very poorly if I don't take careful note of the pauses, the breaks, the continual and abrupt switches from the blasé to the serious, even the solemn—if I don't emphasize the confusing little gestures and expressions that Allan kept making. It was now obvious from his behaviour that he was implying almost embarrassingly that I had a very *specific* reason for taking an interest in Christel. I was oddly irked at him standing back from the discussion at that point, feigning the cruel, obliging stance of the impartial audience. And yet I felt painfully, in a way that confirmed my worst fears, that for him the conversation had now taken a turn that was very far from parody.

"Why not tell you, my dear Allan? It's true that since I met you you've taken me further than I'd often care to admit to myself. You're a strange person, Allan, perhaps exceptional. So I don't blame myself for letting my mind go chasing off after a number of assumptions— wild, romantic—but after all the only ones, yes, *all things considered*, which I could hope would take me further than popular psychology (which we must admit would give too great and even unusual a weight to cynicism here) … "

Allan didn't bat an eyelid but smiled weakly, as if out of politeness.

" … and which in any case seem to be the only ones that let that lighter, more unsettled atmosphere circulate around you—or the image I have of it and the only one I want to keep—those hazy perimeters, that possibility of unseen consequences that appear to be essential. I'll remind you that the white frame that's put round photographs to show them off to advantage is called a *mask*.

"If you like I'll describe *one* of my theories to you. There are others that are possible. But I've got my reasons for starting with this one."

Without a shadow of a smile Allan nodded in agreement.

"There's something of the inexplicable about your stay here, my dear Allan. What one can gather, or guess about you—and in my case I admit it's not very much—doesn't quite fit with life on a sleepy beach, with the constant— let's call it embarrassing—idleness that you visibly trail around with you. It's all too easy to think up excuses for

174

being on holiday—and also too easy to imagine there's some kind of ironic, reasonable alibi. Less experienced people than me—let's set aside any false modesty—haven't been taken in by it, I can tell you.

"So let's assume that in the middle of an exhausting, passionate, unconstrained life you suddenly make some great resolution. From what I know of your character, a resolution of that kind, which can't have any practical purpose whatsoever, absolutely no everyday *success* in mind, which is something you've no time for—instead has some analogy with those sudden ruptures that, in the lives of certain legendary characters, mark the passage to a new *avatar*—the passage from life in the world to the mystic life, from private life to public life, from life in society to the hermitic life. I'm thinking of a *conversion*, a matter of completely changing your image—where, all predictions as to the consequences ruled out, even biographical continuity would suddenly be broken, where according to the mysterious word, 'I' would genuinely become another. I'm thinking of those words—the lives of the saints, Hindu ascetics, great criminals—words which pain biographers and which are littered over certain harrowing pages in the golden legends: '*On that day there began for X … another life*'. Another life? That gives us plenty to dream about.

"The one who's genuinely capable of *converting* has great power. I envisage this power essentially as one of *turning round*, being aware at a glance of the old ruts that have been followed, the ones the ordinary man will continue on until the grave, no more feeling he's a slave than does the carthorse—of letting go the reins of a more or less logical life which keep him in place, bind him hand and foot. Who has the courage to break with everything he's done, everything that's made him what he is, so much so that with the continuity of his personality broken he no longer has any idea what else he can be now, no doubt it could only be a hero, and that's an understatement. But we'll assume you've been this man at least once.

"So let's suppose you've failed here—here as much as elsewhere, isn't that right? Of course the setting doesn't much matter, this one no more than any other: it'll always inevitably be the decor of the seventh day—a strange sort of meteorite out of orbit. You'll do anything. You're capable of anything. The shortcuts, the sheer drops our customary blinkers blind us to, a sense of self-preservation, those unthinking, so-definite choices that the will to live constantly brings about—to you they're just one big journey. You're not committed to anything. You can drain life dry, in all its forms, at any moment. Entirely rational, you're entirely receptive. Not one single chance could pass you by.

"Yes, this setting has everything that a solitary experiment dreams of, the isolation of the mist—the effortless merging with rootless holiday crowds, everything that might have—or must have, isn't that right?—attracted a man who's just had counterfeit keys made and was dreaming about some incredible night of burglary. There's no need to study people too closely here: the easy come easy go of the holidays, the jostle of communal life, like during Carnival, makes every encounter, every experience possible. You have to admit there are very few places where the social guard drops further than on a beach devoted to two months of pusillanimity and idleness. Yes, try as you might it would be hard to find such uncomplicated camaraderie elsewhere. A remarkable idea governs this removal of barriers, the seemingly harmless spring-cleaning of the social order where everything suggests fake seals, forged signatures, the benign official travel permit thrown like a bridge over some bright memories, perhaps."

"A shiver's running down my spine, my dear Gérard. I expect it's the moment the culprit is supposed to lose his nerve. Three pages before the end of a detective novel ... "

"You misunderstand me, Allan; or maybe you understand too well. *There's nothing to make a fuss about* in the riddle I'm suggesting. Everything's so absurd, harmless. Everything lies in what you *imagine* it to be, in a certain oblique, ambivalent power of suggestion, an uncontrolled speculation about man's craving to invent, believe, to construct the complex, the perverse, the mysterious and dangerous. But therein lies the agony and the tragedy. That's where the trap is set, where the killer hides, the killer with clean hands, with, I'm not afraid to say, unsullied hands.

"It *could be*, my dear Allan, that things turn out unexpectedly, that the trap springs itself with my hero sitting in the passenger seat. He's renounced—let's drop that wonderful expression—the world, he's supremely detached from everything. But '*whosoever will lose his life shall save it*'. (Even put into the most diabolical terms that

177

assertion of the Gospel's loses none of its force in my opinion. Even the Devil can't do much about it except charge at it despicably—not put an end to it. See Faust.) Free of everything he finds he's master of everything. Then suddenly from out of voluntary ruin his ultimate chance inevitably appears. Having abdicated he becomes king.

"For one reason or other he probably wasn't at liberty to break off all social ties first. So wherever he goes he finds he's clouding the issue. His partners are thwarted, one by one they show their hand. He changes the scale of values. He complicates the game. That's not to say he cheats. He's simply playing a different game, whose rules no one can work out. He arouses flurries of incomprehension around him. He wins every time: he's not in the least bothered whether he wins *here* or not.

"Such slight of hand probably wouldn't be to everyone's taste. But as ill-disposed as they might be, the most intelligent ones are aware of the futility, the vulgarity of standard defences. *That would be too easy.* They're quite taken with the game. You summon them to *your* territory. They follow you unsuspectingly. Haven't you earned their gratitude if nothing else? They're grateful to you for giving them *a change of air.* Doesn't mountain air exhilarate before it kills? In the most vulnerable people your invisible ray causes a inexhaustible outflow of dreams, of vague elation. I'm thinking of those graceful animals deep down in ocean trenches which are forced by lack of oxygen to grow floaty, branch-like gills, those little parasols of flesh, light as gauze, which the slightest breath of air would tear if they came up out of the deep.

"Do I need to say it? There's a young woman in this. Already very vulnerable, affectionate, heroic, romantic. You're loved."

"Don't you think the joke has gone a bit too far? I'll ask you—and be kind enough to note that I'm asking *seriously*—if you're serious. If I saw fit I *could* find the joke offensive."

"No, you won't be offended. At the point we're at you can't take offence anymore." (I think I was nearly shouting—for some time all this talking had been making me feel unusually eloquent.) "I hope you don't mind me saying, but you've let me go much too far now to not be an accessory. You've *committed* yourself to letting me continue.

"No, you won't be offended. You lost the right to be offended a long time ago, because" (I went on) "we've got to the stage where things begin to go wrong. It's actually very amusing." (In heaven's name why was I putting on a show of cynicism? Yes, why?) "We can laugh about it if you like, Allan; yes, all caution aside, let's laugh like gods. It's too comical."

At this point, cigarette wedged in the corner of his mouth, Allan gave me a frosty look, amused, faintly contemptuous—and I suddenly felt like a drunken serf when he's looked up and down disdainfully by the son of a prince, the son of a king, by one of the Equals.

"I don't think this familiarity is wholly justified. To speak to me on equal terms it's not enough to understand. You have to *pay*."

"I see what you mean, but I haven't said all I've got to say yet. Because in the end it might be that I don't have to pay at all.

"You're a gambler, Allan. Yes, you're a gambler, so without doubt you'll understand. I was thinking that one good game would actually be possible for my hero, an extremely great temptation. *Give chance its head* for a moment. Relax the relentless pressure of the trap he's set so deliberately, so heroically, use some *cunning*, just *to see*, while holding onto the trump cards until they have to be redeemed. With the vague idea that maybe they won't have to be played.

"Prosaically, you could imagine a poker player who starts a new game without looking at his hand.

"Have you ever wondered what a terrible temptation it might be for a god to become human? In the end does the incarnation represent anything other than a defeat (which very few people escape) when faced with the greatest of temptations? To act on both stages at once. One foot in the world of fate, the other in the world of chance—what wild ecstasy! To stand on both sides of the mirror at once. We've all thought of it at least once in our lifetime, and in our dreams we've theoretically staked our lives on it to give vent to our omnipotence. Julien Sorel delights in the thought of his execution—and after all he turns it to his advantage. Remember: *You can't not remember*. '*He followed the tracks of every tear on that lovely face*'. Which of us hasn't rejoiced with pleasure and self-satisfaction at the thought of the tears that will run down the cheeks of our own flesh and blood after we're dead."

For the first time I saw a glint of anger in Allan's eyes. "You're disgraceful."

"I'm right. You know that better than anyone."

But he calms down already. He tries very hard to be calm. Yes, this man's composure is amazing. His voice is low and whistling again—but graceful—yes, bearable.

"Very well. But you were talking about redeeming things. And that, dear fellow, is where your conclusion seems to fall down. Either this redemption is irreversible, fixed *come what may*—in which case you're not really playing for fun anymore, you're not really *playing* at all—I think the example of Julien Sorel applies particularly here (Allan winked in an unsettling way) or, as you so rightly pointed out, it's a piece of dramatic fiction aimed at giving the very lowest-quality individual the illusion of playing some tragic game to which his means would never allow him access. Would you reduce this 'hero' to whom you've attached such great significance to this painful alternative?

"Does the man I'm thinking of even know himself what he'll eventually choose? Carry on playing? Or throw in his hand? He's managed to make the game more exciting. He's living though an exhilarating period in his life. Can't he accept the chances that the situation offers him without counting the cost?"

"My dear Gérard, your hero is a devil turned hermit. He's calculating the petty little benefits he's going to get from his conversion. Forgive me for thinking for a moment there that you were serious."

"Let me make myself clear, Allan. This is no joking matter now. It's probably a matter of something vastly more tragic than either you or I perhaps imagine. Gregory left so as not to see what's going to happen here. Perhaps that's news to you."

"You're not telling me anything new."

"Another moral tale. Like me you've read the story of the young man who manages to seduce a young woman, the only love of his life, on the formal understanding that they both commit suicide afterwards. But *afterwards* he thinks life is fine and wonderful and doesn't kill himself. Doubtless he's not breaking his word at all. Because who can make promises in the name of the man who comes *afterwards*—the one who calmly bestrides the conquered body of the woman like the frontiers of a new world, a newly-enchanted world.

"*Now* I'm going to follow up on your 'devilish' comparison, and I'll look you in the eye and say this. The resolution might have been genuine. I think it was, I'm sure of it. But isn't it one of the devil's final, most formidable chances, quickly changing his plans, to suddenly show the saint, after the event, the enormous *advantages* his conversion provides for him?"

A pale sun, an unreal sun came up over the crest of the waves. With its stiff, gnarled, washed-out joints Brittany's great gloomy body appears from the mist. What a lonely coastline! Had we come so far already? The exhilarating cry of the gulls, so disorienting, falls from high up in their wild domain, making its raucous sound carry further, last longer. What views might these misty porticos vaguely festooned with seabirds—this hardened coastline—open on to?

What a strange morning, shot through with pallid, wandering, sightless rays like the pencil beam from a lighthouse which you'd like to hold in your fingers. What a time of sober mystery—muffled, downy with layers of translucent cotton wool, with long, clear, yawning vistas like the crooked windows of a house made of snow. Desolate isolation. The cold gentle water, so still between the small cracks in the rocks with its tiny, artless creatures. The cold watery sand. The pure grey salt that scours this primitive carapace of every stain. You'd like to set off from here on some hopeless voyage, a great departure, to tread this unkind, unwelcoming land for the last time.

How hard it is for this ground to endure life, how it expels it! Here more than elsewhere you could, should think harder about your reasons for staying, ask yourself exactly what your chances are.

"I'll ask you something, Gérard. Did you come to talk to me this morning as a friend—sincere, unbiased—or did someone—I'd rather not name names—ask you to make these … enquiries? I'll warn you now, an awful lot depends on your answer."

"I can't answer that."

What a piercing look he gave me! And for the second time that fear, that same foreboding shot through me.

"So what do you see, looking at me like that?"

"But … I don't know. Perhaps the face of that temptation you were just talking about.

"You frighten me, Allan. I've sensed it since I've been here: you're on the brink of something irreversible.

183

I probably can't do anything for you, but it would be hard for me to think I've done something *against* you."

"Don't worry, you won't be held accountable. In the limited sense of the word of course, where it involves struggles of conscience as interesting as they're a matter of form."

"You know of another sense?"

"Yes. So do you. Otherwise you'd have spared me this somewhat niggardly lecture. I can tell you this: I don't have, I've never had a problem with my conscience. But responsible, that I certainly am. Not for my faults. But for my successes, my failures, my chances. For the unbroken line of chances that sustain me, run through, shape, impale me and which one day, without my knowledge and after my flimsy *wishes* have crumbled, will write its *test*—as different from and as unsuspected by my self-willed me as a skeleton is to a living body—its testimony, as the geologists strongly advise, me as I am, as I would always have been. If you like, not about my behaviour but my *path* on this earth."

"You believe in the man of destiny so much?"

"Your irony has no effect on me. I'm going to provoke it again. Ask Napoleon: don't you feel the responsibility for the death of millions of people weighing on you? You're just met with a shrug. Monstrous insensitivity? Lack of moral sense? Simply this: *it's no concern of his.* His responsibility lies on another plane: the painstaking, tentative completion of some incredible trajectory which he senses is his mission to carve in fiery letters in the ground. Even during his lifetime he'd have felt far more *bound* by the most commonplace elegy ('*born on an island, died on an island*') than by the most categorical imperative."

"I could be Napoleon on that point. Any man could."

"That's unspeakable arrogance."

"Or perhaps it's utmost humility. The term used to describe it is totally immaterial."

"Don't you think that what the Church calls a damned person must feel more or less like that?"

"So you'll have me believe there's this permanent hell inside a person, because he has no qualms about getting a sense of pleasure and pride from it. Or maybe it's only in this rut that he opens up for himself as he goes along that he feels free. What does he say to his first love? 'You're the one I had to meet. That's how it is. It couldn't be any other way.' He claims to be and feels human. Perhaps a man only feels truly human, truly free, at those rare moments in his life which he thinks could have been prophesied."

"You want to speak Christian language to me: well, believe me, even the Gospel doesn't have much to ease people's consciences. '*But woe to that man by whom the offence cometh*'—a phrase like that doesn't exactly encourage sophistry, it's aimed less at the driving force than at the *instrument*. Humanity regarded, and struck, as an instrument."

"All right. I won't try touching that cord any more— who knows, maybe I wouldn't do that with enough conviction either. But I came here this morning to ask you a question, and I'm not going to leave without having done so."

"Go on. Let's have done with it, yes, that would be for the best."

"I'm going to silence my personal assumptions and what might be just idle curiosity now. But here you are, faced with a *fact*. You've aroused an interest in the young woman whose name I mentioned which isn't focused solely on you as a person—but on some revelation beyond you, some promise of which, rightly or wrongly, she sees you as the medium, the bearer. I think that what I'm trying to express in this terse way is perfectly clear enough for you."

"Perhaps."

"So here's my question: faced with the *consequences*, which could be unpredictable, this *role*, which is probably beyond you—do you think you have the right to take it on?"

"And why not?"

"Fine. I don't think I've got any more to say to you."

We left each other in a heavy silence.

24th August

DOLORÉS HAS COME BACK. She's the one that that letter predicted.

Gérard's diary ends here. The information he gave me—for I often questioned him at length, passionately, in detail—certain parts of letters that he passed on to me, as well as accounts from some of the guests at the Hôtel des Vagues, have enabled me to complete the intrigue that can be seen vaguely taking shape in the pages of this diary—and whose outcome still leaves me sunk in feelings of mysterious uncertainty even as I write these lines.

1st September—a Sunday that year—was traditionally the date of the grand fancy dress ball of the season at the Hôtel des Vagues. The day had been dull and overcast beneath a canopy of cloud heavy with a storm that was slow in coming, a delay that made the sticky, unbearable afternoon seem to pass more slowly. In the preparations for the party—the high point of the season, the day after which the hotel would begin to empty—there had been something feverish, excessive. Since Dolorés got back Allan had barely left her side, and his relationship with the rest of the little group had become more and more distant. During this whole period he apparently carried on gambling heavily. And now the season was nearly over, and some people were beginning to sense that these celebrations, in which against his normal habits Allan had promised to take part, wouldn't end without some bizarre incident.

It was in Gérard particularly that this edginess became more noticeable. Solemn, reticent, cutting conversations short and often unusually abrupt, he shut himself away in his room for long periods, pacing up and down, chain-smoking. The only company he seemed able to bear was Henri's—and in conversations with him, as if obsessed, he constantly referred to the party—"the party with no tomorrow". He himself had difficulty defining this semi-hypnotic state, the indecisiveness in which he was plunged all week long. His feelings about Allan remained highly ambivalent. "I couldn't leave him," he told me later, "I only had to see him from the window, leaving the hotel—because I watched him, watched him closely, patiently—for my room to suddenly seem oppressive, and despite myself my legs would carry me off to where I'd vaguely seen him heading. I hoped for nothing, not even an encounter. The days were mild and grey that week, the sea unusually still. Sometimes I lay on the dunes and, putting my head back—any other occupation suddenly striking me as pitifully futile—let my eyes follow the line of clouds skimming over the tips of the quivering grass. And the memory of my last conversation with Allan constantly came back to me—with stubborn, stupid determination I kept going back in my mind over such-and-such an intonation of a phrase, some indefinable timbre in his voice that suddenly assumed the significance of a code, a password. Because however doubtful I may still have been I wasn't any less certain that Allan had told me *everything*, that apart from polite, unimportant small talk our relationship was now a permanently closed book—and that from now on the game would be played elsewhere. There was scandal in the air, already fed by nervous excitement, so different from the relaxed enjoyment of a normal party, making the faces that day a more vivid shade of pink, that unhealthy, changeable complexion that burns the cheeks of people with fever. All day long preparations for the party had been going full swing in the hotel that was suddenly decorated with tall green plants, where noises became denser in the hothouse half-light. More than anything the thought of a *masked* ball made me uneasy. The secret of what costumes the little gang were going to wear hadn't leaked out. Instinct told me that Allan now couldn't not find some dubious, exciting invitation in this party, one of those *chances* he was so fond of, to at last (and I'd been driven to point this out to him so clumsily) *openly* put on the mask that he'd been wearing theoretically from the moment he arrived. And I sensed that that irrepressible liking of his for the man-to-man challenge, for violent provocation—like the matador who with a stamp of his foot, outright and in a harsh voice, summons the bull within reach of his blade—was bound to make him *unmask* this very evening. Yes, in this world without bearings, out of its frame, suddenly abandoned to muffled drifting, to a frozen and shimmering escape through time, constrained by heavy trains, gold embroidery, antique silks, to an imperceptibly greater formality, in this unreal invitation, so accurate in effortlessly grafting itself onto the living, this world of ghosts, concealing any too-genuine gesture with the harmless iridescence of a stage direction, smoothing out the corners, stage-managing the transitions, weaving those virtuoso *conjuring tricks* that he secretly knows so well—perhaps he'd just been waiting to choose, to identify his *true territory.*"

At eight in the evening, after a quick dinner—doors closed on rooms full of fevered footsteps, jewellery jingling and hairpins handled as if under a spell, the rustle of trains, the excited, muted bustle of the ambush and the lure, where that potent hypnotism, the faint sharp jingling frenzy, that slightly deadly and solemn formality of the grandest evenings builds up—doors behind which every women caught alone would for a second look like some lunatic rehearsing a murder scene in the mirror—the hotel seemed to briefly doze, unseeing and silent beside a beach that twilight had emptied of its belongings, abandoned to the last flights, the lazy cries of seabirds in the oblique light from the sea.

Night falls over the bay under a blanket of heavy cloud, over the oily sea. The beach is empty. From his balcony Gérard watches a fisherwoman on rocks that just break the surface of the water at the far end of the bay, and who lingers round the clear pools, remote, with the slow tortuous progress of an insect, fascinated by the empty languor, the yawning lethargy of the sun over the sea. The reassuring weary world of daytime seems to be expiring out there, to be stuck in the sand along with her. The sudden sound of a brass section comes from the big lobby like a muffled explosion: the party has begun.

"I have to admit I'm still puzzled," Christel was saying to a stylish young man dressed in the latest thing from

1900. "Mind you, you're not playing fair. The rules say that to avoid mix-ups every guest has to wear something connected with the character they've come as."

"Sorry dear lady, but etiquette requires that I leave the most identifiable part of my costume in the cloakroom. Otherwise no doubt you'd have rallied round it like the famous white plume."[7]

"So might I … ?"

"My beaver hat. I'm Lafcadio. May I have the pleasure?"

They danced. Suntanned, Christel made a well-baptised and very proper Atala. Around her neck was her little gold crucifix.

"Wherever do you think Kersaint got the notion of filling his hotel with heroes from novels and poems tonight? He's a lovely man—but this hare-brained scheme is most unlike him."

"I'll let you into a secret: it was Gérard's idea. Of course to Kersaint every word he says is gospel truth."

"Is he here?"

"Over there, dancing with the rather ageing Charlotte. That dolman suits him. Grey I think, probably Russian. I'm afraid I'm as clueless as one can be about their literature."

In his officer's dolman from the Austerlitz campaign Gérard imagined he was everyone's idea of Prince Andrei from *War and Peace*.

The music stopped: the couples mingled. There was already quite a crowd—virtually every guest from the hotel. The evening was getting lively.

"Monsieur de Rastignac? All right then, 'here's to the two of us'. But before you carry your conquests any further, take me to that little anachronism of a bar ... I've got a frightful thirst."

"Jacques looks as if he's at his first dance. See? He's terrified, drinking to bolster his self-confidence. If Rastignac is here tonight it's because he's escaped from Vauquer's boarding house."

"Do be quiet, you malicious gossip. I think you wanted to make us all look like something out of some literary journal for academics just to give yourself a target for your irony. Because all this is your idea isn't it?"

"And you've turned it into your triumph, dear Countess. All the barbarity of the steppe joins me tonight at the feet of the dark beauty of the Midi."

The cruel, slightly primitive little touches in Irène's Spanish costume brought out her full-bodied beauty to perfection. Heavy yet graceful, reinforced by her dark, dignified complexion like an impregnable city, a thoroughbred, a princess of the stage, she held the almost regal train of the Countess Almaviva in a steely grip.

"It's only your good taste getting its reward. Don't forget it was you who recommended this Spanish costume to me."

"But there's more than one person who'll be thinking more of Chérubin tonight."

Flustered, Irène gave him a pointed, puzzled look. But the other dancers crushed them against each other— hesitantly they put their arms round one another's waist.

"I wonder who Allan will come as tonight."

The question made half a dozen heads turn.

"Apparently Jacques is the only one in on the secret."

"So it's been well-kept then."

"Even from you? From a woman?"

"Would you prefer me to find that tactless or offensive?"

"*Very* ladylike! We're obviously fated to exchange witticisms tonight."

"But I've asked myself that question too."

"And out of pure generosity you've extended it to the beauty who enthrals his nights."

"Don't be spiteful."

He lowered his voice.

"I'm waiting for Allan and Dolorés with more than just curiosity."

"Oh, come on my dear. He's going to hor-ri-fy us, it goes without saying. The great shudder. Brr! It makes me shiver already. Banquo's ghost, or Hamlet's noble father, or even the Mask of the Red Death. And with the Bleeding Nun on his arm. Someone who sits up all night in churches, just imagine! He must know everything about the spirit world."

"There's a grain of sense in your ravings, my darling. You're not as ironic as you'd like to be."

Henri had come over, eyes uneasy, darting.

"What have you got against him?"

"I like people … "

"There they are!" Henri announced in such a stricken voice that Iréne and Gérard turned to look at the same moment.

Cheerful, in the middle of a lively discussion, Allan and Dolorés had just appeared at the foot of the stars. Allan, so very elegant, wore the costume of the young lions of 1830—trousers with understraps, exuberant waistcoat, flowing cravat—Dolorés the full-length hooded cloak with velvet ribbons, broderie anglaise, a bell-shaped dress—utterly simple, no jewels—of the romantic *grisettes*. Reunited, bound together by a graceful flow of words, with that affectionate, touching tilt of the head where phrases seem about to turn into a kiss, they seemed to float like apparitions—and the footlights came on around them again, suddenly drawing people's gazes as imperiously as if a spotlight had picked them out in a darkened auditorium. On one side of their costumes, over the heart, provocative, brazen as a freshly picked flower, was a large bloodstain.

"The lovers of Montmorency," said Jacques matter-of-factly.

If Irène's face expressed anything at that point it was that she refused to believe her eyes.

"What are you saying?"

"Come on Irène, it's a well-known poem by Vigny. Two young lovers who've decided to 'have done with life' go off to Montmorency for the weekend. At the end of the weekend they commit suicide together. That's all."

Rather embarrassed to see his words met with stony silence, Jacques broke off—on his left seeing Gérard suddenly turn into a statue, on his right Irène with a malicious smile on her face—Henri pale, grey-lipped.

"Well … it's in pretty appalling taste," put in Henri, hesitantly—anything being suddenly more bearable than silence.

"I don't know why he was so insistent about the blood-stain. He said it was absolutely essential, that it was the 'symbolic attribute'. He's been very odd for quite a while."

Jacques was ashamed of this abortive entrance as if it were a joke that had fallen flat. But by now Allan was there, eyes shining, effusive, obviously in high spirits.

"What do you think of the idea, Gérard? So poetic isn't it? And I'll tell you a secret, it's a subtle, quite particular thought dedicated to all of you. People don't read Vigny nowadays—as Wilde would say. So here's my chance—my word yes, that's what I told myself!—to give a knowing wink to those *so very* cultured friends of ours. A rallying cry for the *happy few*.[8] It's *so* exciting isn't it my dear Gérard, it *really* livens up a party (he gripped his arm) to feel you've got *fellow conspirators* somewhere among the indifferent crowd."

Hurriedly, Henri asked Dolorés to dance. Irène had quickly slipped out of range …

"Do you really think it's in the best taste to come to a party dressed as death in all his finery?"

"Worthwhile reminder, my dear Gérard—a worthwhile reminder! I assume we're all mortals here. You know there was never any lack of that sort of spice at banquets in the last days of the Roman Empire. 'Eat, drink and be merry, for tomorrow we die.' You know, Gérard, I feel terribly decadent tonight."

"You're out of place tonight, I can assure you of that. You've no right to go putting on such a ghastly performance. There's something obscene about all this exhibitionism. You'd best leave, I tell you Allan."

"That confirms the high opinion I have of your intelligence, Gérard. Here, I'll announce it in the presence of witnesses" (he raised his voice in a shocking way. He'd clearly decided not to stand on ceremony tonight—there was an unnervingly mischievous twinkle in his eye), "here is a man of learning. There's nothing to suggest this room is overflowing with them. Hello Jacques! Your costume is sensational. But believe me, Candide would have suited you better."

Gradually a wave of embarrassment, indescribable awkwardness spread out around Allan. It was as if in some obscure way everyone guessed that tonight, protected by an invisible talisman, he could *do whatever he liked*, tear off the masks and expose the real faces. From now on an uneasy malaise, as if around the sickbed of someone whose condition is constantly at crisis-point, would reign over this false, faithless night until morning came. Under cover of this false, sultry light of dawn, of these endangered festivities, suddenly free of having to put people off the scent it landed here in a decisive surprise attack with all the baleful impudence of a ghost, borne on the wings of ease, of some fabulous complicity, and paced through the rooms wearing Gyges's ring on its finger.

"Come along, Prince," he said suddenly. "Discretion, silence! We'll go and plead our case as harmless spirits so we can run off with Christel."

Gérard stopped, put his hand on Allan's arm and looked at him calmly, sadly.

"You're on your own now, Allan. Wherever you're going—and you know it—I can't and don't wish to follow you."

"Isn't the night peaceful, Christel—look at it. There are the stars from your dream, and the sea you're not frightened of now. No, I'm not feverish, there's nothing to be afraid of—I feel released, calm. I'm with you and I feel good. Give me your hand, let's walk under the trees for a moment. It's a beautiful night. It's true the stars are like in your dream, like a promise—they shine beyond the darkness. Such purity is hard to imagine. Nothing can go wrong tonight, can it?"

"Of course not, Allan. Why do you need me to reassure you? Are you like a child, afraid of the dark?"

"Yes, sometimes I'm afraid. But let's leave that, those are sad things. Tonight I'm with you. For a few minutes I'm far away from the others—the others don't matter anymore. Haven't you ever noticed: sometimes on a road, a beach, you see a man and a woman walking hand in hand—and you sense that even within arm's reach they're suddenly more cut off from each other, more remote than all these stars—more untouchable. Anything can last between two people for the space of a few seconds, for two or three foolish phrases, as long they revolve around each other, make their timid, planet-like music. Move one of your stars aside and make room for me, Christel. Let's go over to the terrace that looks out to sea."

They went a little way without speaking. Sometimes a snatch of music slipped out of the open windows, but by now there was a cold night breeze, an alarm signal from the exhausted leaves, the confused shadows of the trees; the night, untiring, was looking out for its own on the threshold of a house under siege. Allan slipped a coat over Christel's shoulders.

"Is it really just the two of us now, Allan?"

"Yes. At this moment."

He took her hand in both of his and stared at her for a while.

"Why are you looking at me like that? In such a hard, fixed way? I'm quite frightened."

"I'm looking at you like the one who arrives at the eleventh hour. I was so afraid I'd miss you. These holidays are so short, a time suspended, ageless—like a secret offering, a lure for the gods of fate. But everything comes to an end. I've met you Christel, and that stroke of luck is a blessing for me. But soon I'll be leaving."

"You're telling me this in such a hard voice. It sounds more like a threat than a piece of news. Do you think I haven't said to myself, repeated—every day, every hour—that you were going to leave."

There was a delicious quiver of terror and delight in Christel's voice. Allan took her hand, kissed it again and again, fervently.

"Whatever happens I've heard those words, Christel, and they'll stay in my heart forever."

He looked at her face transformed by the moon, floating calmly over the night, breathtakingly, heart-stoppingly beautiful—lost in pained surprise.

"I'm yours, Allan, you know that—if you want me. Even now, at this moment."

She gazed into his eyes.

" … Even if there's no tomorrow."

There was a long silence. Christel could feel Allan's hand shaking.

"Even if there is no tomorrow?"

Christel looked at him. His face was changing. Bitter irony suddenly contorted his mouth.

" … Or especially if there's no tomorrow?"

"My God, what do you mean?"

He moved away from her with a bitter smile.

"I'll tell you a story, Christel. There was once a man who sold his soul to the Devil, who in return let him win the heart of a young woman. Then, won over by the purity of her love he thought this love would save him, set him free from the trap. But he realized how much stronger the Devil was, because it was now *her* in her innocence who was tightening the noose of the trap, it was no longer *him* but the one he'd signed the pact with who'd made himself the object of her love, and it was now his lot to *become* the damned face that he'd only put on as a mask. A rather frightening story, isn't it?"

Christel looked at him without replying, eyes vacant.

" … but logical, how very logical! And you can refer the one who can unravel the *tangled outcome* of this little tale to me. To me personally."

And with a wild laugh Allan disappeared towards the lobby.

"You're so frightened of ghosts, Gérard! You'll have me doubting Allan's high opinion of your judgement. This costume seems perfectly innocuous to me."

"Was the macabre allusion your idea?"

"I think it was both of ours. I don't think I have to tell you we're very close. Yes, sometimes our innermost thoughts suddenly coincide. It's impressive isn't it, this instinctive communication of ours."

She stared at him with visible insolence. Abruptly, Gérard turned away. With the moon behind a cloud the garden suddenly got very dark, submerged in a damp breath of wind. You could hear the peaceful sound of the sea on the rocks. Along with the middle of the night came a sudden chill. It was that solemn moment of repose and expectation when the stars start to give way to morning.

"You're so safe, Dolorés. You seem so sheltered—protected by an invisible shield."

"I think it's just my costume that protects me. At a dance like this it's easy to take yourself for a god paying an incognito visit to the world in your grey cloak, don't you think."

"You've got imagination."

"I don't usually really feel I'm in the world. And for me this is a beautiful night. I have the feeling I've come back to see friends after my death. Everything's so strange around us—it doesn't take much imagination to think we're at a gathering of ghosts."

"I still feel very much alive, Dolorés. But since you arrived, you and Allan—and how strange to hear you say out loud what I've sensed more than once—yes, I could go along with that allegory more easily."

Dolorés gave an absent, unwavering smile.

"I read somewhere that death is a secret society. It really makes you think. What for most people is just the end, a *stopgap*—and that's an understatement—for others might be a vocation."

"I've sometimes thought that too, and never as much as tonight. And like all vocations it's infectious."

Again Dolorés smiled, softly, in an almost unreal way. She seemed to shake off a troublesome thought.

" I don't think there's much to be afraid of."

Gérard's voice came from out of the darkness—harsh, impassioned, sombre.

"Don't play with fire. You can't know that."

She took his head in her hands and with a radiant, smiling expression held it in front of her face.

"Oh come on, Gérard, you're highly intelligent. Don't think I'm making fun of you. What you admitted just now touched me enormously. But this is all impossible. Don't hold it against me Gérard; just remember me. I've given you the best possible proof that I trust you. But don't get mixed up in a game that's not yours to play. You know very well that all that's impossible."

"I love you, Dolorés."

"You're a very dear friend. And you know enough

about me to realize I'm not just saying that to fob you off. Goodbye, Gérard, although who knows—maybe we'll see each other again? But now we have to part."

"I can't do anything with you: the definition of despair. But I'll remember you as I love you."

She kissed his forehead.

"Goodbye then. And remember the watchword of secret societies."

"Which is?"

"The secret."

"Another waltz, Irène?"

Jacques leant right up against her face, her teeth, the moist lips the very image of unsubtle desire, only saved from coarseness by the noble touches of its magnificent matt sheen—that triumphant complexion that withstands the dull fatigue of four in the morning.

She laughed close to his lips, a provocative laugh, barely suppressed, feeling him quiver with desire against her.

"Really another waltz? I'm so tired?"

"It's the last one, Irène. Please, don't turn me down."

She kept up her undecided pout. Then suddenly her eyes shone with a strange gleam.

"I'll let you have this dance on condition you give me something in return."

"The head of John the Baptist?"

Beneath the lowered mask the teeth shone again. A primitive charm, which flesh alone wasn't capable of recognizing tonight, came from the voluptuous face.

"Less. You're my friend, tell me all you know about Allan."

"But, Irène … ? You make an odd Salomé! I don't know much about him. I've got absolutely nothing to hide. Why ask such a simple thing with so much seriousness—as if we were suddenly talking about betraying him?"

Irène gave a cold, impudent smile.

"My dear young Jacques, don't cloak your jealousy in the colours of high-minded friendship. You don't know how comical you are."

"I couldn't say anything now even if I wanted to. No, I'm not jealous, but I don't like questions with a threat behind them."

"Have it your own way. I'm dead on my feet. See me up to my room."

As they left the bright light of the lobby the long, deserted corridors seemed submerged in semi-darkness— the cold night air of the sea suddenly gripped the throat. They walked quickly, noiselessly—thieves making a silent getaway. Far from the music, the lights, alone with this violent Irène and her energetic strides, a lump came to Jacques's throat, again he was seized with self-consciousness, overwhelming shyness.

Outside her door Irène turned round. Jacques felt himself blush to the roots of his hair and, looking down, sick with uncertainty, he clung to her hand like a drowning man to a piece of wreckage.

"Allan's room is almost opposite. Let's go in for a second," she whispered, brushing his forehead distractedly with her lips.

Lifeless, Jacques let himself be led. In the dark sombre room a faint square of light came through the half-open door and fell on the blue coat, the weapons which glinted faintly. The corners shrunk back in translucent darkness. Here and there a ray of hostile light caught a hinge, a lock. It was like a shuttered lantern, a hasty thought which with a terrified crack pierces a silence as tightly-woven as cloth. Time weighed heavily, hung round their shoulders. In her great, sombre, stately dress, eyes unaccustomed to the dark Irène stood upright, the black silk mask blending her face dramatically with the night.

"You're crazy, Irène," muttered Jacques, suddenly calling her '*tu*', dragging at her hand, losing his nerve.

In the darkness he heard a calm whisper.

"Let go of me. Isn't that his desk?"

"Yes, but let's go. Let's go, please. What do you want to do?"

There was a sound of nimble fingers skimming over drawers, handles, moving papers with swift, unsettling animal deftness. And yet the tall figure leaning forward was motionless. Jacques felt himself shiver slightly.

"Look!" The low voice, as if submerged in extraordinary childhood waves by the pressure of intense, naked curiosity, was suddenly so close to him that he gave a start. Face against his, almost oblivious to his presence, Irène slowly held up a revolver by its barrel.

"Irène, let's go! Come on, please, let's go!"

The low whisper came again, very close, calm, almost impersonal.

"You're such a child! There's nothing to be frightened of. Allan's downstairs, dancing with Dolorés. It's amusing in here isn't it? Don't you like it in the dark?"

"Irène—not here, no, please—not here."

"Come on … "

She pulled him close, onto the couch, rubbing her breasts gently against his chest. Below her black mask, a faint drop of liquid light on her dark lips, with savage stillness, with the slow movements of a sleepwalker, she leant her face over him. Jacques felt a violent flood of desire spring up in him.

" … Kiss me."

Wrapped in moist, satiating warmth he yielded.

"It's dawn. Daylight's coming up over the sea."

Among the by now fewer couples, the snatches of already rarer talking, clinking glasses, into the large dining room there suddenly came that slightly mournful solemnity, like fingers unentwining, parties that draw to a close. Sometimes there was silence, heavier for a second, uninhabited, melancholy, then chased away by a burst of laughter that came back compulsively, prowling round like a bee, sure of being the strongest in the end. And with every door that slammed, every couple that slipped away, a wave of cold air swept through the room, and bare shoulders shivered in its slipstream, so long in passing. Out of the windows that looked out to sea a faint grey line was just appearing, stretched low over the horizon.

At a table by the window Dolorés, Gérard, Christel, Henri and Jacques were having a last drink. Standing with his back turned, Allan gazed absently out to sea. Strained, shivery, motionless, for a while they stayed silent as if listening to the seconds fly past, time suddenly irreversible, the last minutes slipping away more quickly like grains of sand in an hourglass. Something was about to fall apart.

With a vague sound of instruments being packed away the musicians left the platform. Almost despite themselves the few remaining voices dropped. Taking refuge against the walls they watched the empty space that was ousting them get bigger in the middle of the room, a steppe of bare parquet that suddenly surfaced from beneath gentle waves, gradually *took hold*, coming closer and closer like a sheet of ice, giving the large room a look of yawning nakedness, the stillness of a frosty winter day. Morning seeped in through the windows like water through a cracked shell, turned their vivid glad rags pale as if withering them—whorls of cigar smoke arranged in stately strata, heavy scrolls just below the ceiling, gave this emptiest of rooms—now deserted after all the mighty cannonades of brass—the grandeur of a household down to its last penny.

The last couples left. Casually Allan went across to the open piano, slowly sat down and, first distractedly, then passionately, gloomily, began to play a nocturne. The final notes echoed, slow to die away, mysterious, uneven, uncertain, and still they listened, souls dissolving, lost in painful drowsiness. In the tall empty room morning was

207

on the rise, flooding in like the sea. In a corridor a clock chimed, shrill, slow.

Slightly solemn, slightly pale, Henri raised his glass.

"To holidays past—and holidays to come."

"To the lovely Christel and Dolorés."

"To all of you: to Christel, Henri, Gérard, Jacques— long life and happiness!"

Standing on the edge of the platform, one hand on Dolorés' shoulder, Allan raised his glass.

"Here we are, alone in this room. In a way I believe in the ghosts of morning. It's the time the angels come down, the moment for bad dreams. Without doubt a spirit has joined this little group of ours. Let's not drive it away. I invite this unknown ghost to sit with us. I drink to the health of the one that brought us together."

Vichy

September abruptly emptied the Hôtel des Vagues again. In the dining room the tables soon thinned out, the corridors drifted off to sleep. Shutters banged on the windows of villas, and for most of the now shorter mornings the beach stood empty. Then came the autumn gales, exhausting, seemingly endless, and all along the shore there was nothing to be heard but the glorious, breathless sound of the great pinewoods—and with the now cold, longer nights endangered houses huddled up behind faded fences. Yet neither Henri, Jacques, Christel, Gérard, Allan nor Dolorés thought of leaving. The days flew by, always shorter, irretrievable—and the Hôtel des Vagues seemed to stay open just for them, enjoying a secret late autumn season, a more astute maturity, a choicer, more bitter fruit after a shameful retirement. Out of season, out of time, facing a horizon progressively consumed by mist, the indecisive days flowed past for them—cut off from the world by the now all-powerful rumbling of the sea—and there they stayed, bogged down, prolonging week by week a stay that became increasingly unjustifiable, drifting limply through the days, waiting blindly, with exhausting indecision. For each of them, each of these days that a *timetable* never disrupted, each of these ageless days, so obviously, so irrevocably condemned to being the *last* had something of a wild, free flavour about it; and every morning on these unoccupied days, uprooted from time—like a condemned man's reprieve, a schoolboy's holiday lengthened at the last minute by a miraculous death, illness—suddenly seemed wide open to secret possibilities; as if, as far removed from these humdrum holidays as from a string of everyday tasks, to them these days suddenly seemed—out of proportion, ominous, almost overpoweringly full—to be the only ones they really won back from death.

So the days drifted by, more and more empty, more and more idle. And between the survivors of the beautiful summer, on this faded beach that was suddenly so extraordinary as winter drew on, an unspoken intimacy now sprung up. In the dining room, or sometimes after dinner on a cold night when there was a fire, all of a sudden, disorienting, the nostalgic atmosphere of a winter evening with friends would creep in. The night would pass, full and slow, and gathered round the fire they would listen, listen to Allan talking, ears suddenly attuned to the closer, more sovereign crash of the waves, watching the great dancing shadows that the fire cast on the wall. In the depths of a closed-off night it was as if they'd suddenly been transported to the wardroom of a ship trapped in winter ice floes—a ghostly pause in time, as if frozen by frost—and from then on there was nothing that mattered in the passing of the days on this open expanse—except the gratifying presence of the captain on board and, suddenly, totally detached from all else, all moorings loosed on this ship sailing across smooth open plains, the birth of *another order*, a miraculous order …

Only Irène seemed to escape the deadly charms of the season's end. Apparently she'd already insisted to Henri several times, sharply, passionately, that they should leave. One afternoon the sounds of a short, sudden altercation, slamming doors, violent, fiery threats shook the hotel— and then it was calm again—that flat unreal calm that exists even in the heart of a hurricane, a lull more *impending* than the storm itself, extending all the way to the horizon among the furious battening of the waves.

On the morning of the last day of September, under a clear sky the windows of the hotel opened onto bare moorland gently whitened by the first frost and, as one tiny drop will crystallize a supersaturated solution by falling into it, all at once the dangerous state of tranquillity which till then had bound them in the closest of complicities disappeared—and instantly they woke up.

"Is it possible there's frost already?" Christel said to Gérard from the steps of the lawn as he came back from his morning swim, huddled in a bathrobe.

"Absolutely certain. The water's freezing. The holidays are well and truly over."

"So soon!"

She just stood there on the steps, not moving, like a ploughman watching a violent hailstorm, staring at the faded, changed landscape—still unsure, incredulous at the sight of this disaster.

"Let's sit down for a second, if you don't mind. I've something to say to you."

With her beach umbrella Irène gestured towards a bench screened off from the grounds, close to the terrace overlooking the sea. After the viciously cold morning the afternoon was suddenly delightful. A slight wind made the unwearying pines rustle. Beyond the terrace the sea stretched out, glittering through gaps in the branches; in the amazingly crisp clear air the grand, deserted outline of the bay, the empty beach, opened up like a clearing in the depths of some forgotten wood.

A little formally Allan sat down at the other end of the bench from her.

"I wanted to ask when you plan on leaving."

He gave her a nasty look.

"I don't think there's any mistaking your tone. It's not the friendliest of questions."

"It doesn't claim to be. I think you can guess why I'm asking."

"It'll have something to do with your friend I imagine."

"At least you're honest. It's about her, and others …
You can't stay here. All this has to stop."

"All this … what's that supposed to mean?"

Blazing, she flew at him.

"The scandal of you being here."

"Might I ask what I've done that's so despicable?"

She pulled a derisive face.

"You're above any kind of evidence, and well you know
it. You're too careful—too clever. But you know perfectly
well what I mean."

He gave a poisonous smile.

"I see your friend's interests are very close to your
heart."

"All right. I don't have a problem admitting that. After
all, the disgraceful game you're playing with Christel
doesn't concern me personally. I've got more selfish
motives actually."

"So I've done something to hurt you."

"Me, everybody. You've made this holiday a misery. A
time that was doubly important for me, which decided
everything. I'm newly-married … You enjoy spoiling
everything around you. Nothing grows in your shadow.
People can be happy, get by, make the most of life with
much less than you think, you know. But no! You had
to come and destroy it (she stamped her foot, carried
away, violent, vulgar), spoil it, ruin it—everything that's
possible, normal, so simple. Just with that graveside face
of yours, the face that spells misfortune … "

"I'm quite convinced now that this bizarre curse has
spared you at least."

She gave him a hateful look.

"No, that's right—I'm not in danger. I'm alive, very much alive, so these sophisticated suicide threats leave me cold … "

She was gradually raising her voice—a fading voice, lacking resonance, infuriated.

" … Because after all that's what you've been doing here the entire time, that's what it is. This permanent look of Werther, this masquerade. Oh, you're so *interesting!* And at so little cost. Yes, it's really all too simple!"

"At so little cost?"

"You wouldn't have me believe … "

"Yes I would."

She stared at him, distraught, her face changed. There was a long silence. Then she began to talk again, very quietly.

"You've no right to say such things."

"I see what you mean. But it's you who made me have this unseemly conversation."

She sat up, cheeks burning, eyes bulging, ferocious.

"I didn't mean anything. I didn't intend to mean anything."

"Please yourself. Actually that's *awkward*, isn't it?"

Casually he got up and walked away under the trees. Suddenly evening closed in, the trees in the deserted garden gave a brief shudder at the sound of waves approaching—the tide was coming in. A cloud threw a veil of shadow over these grounds suddenly surrounded by uproar and silence, a sheet of grey dust in which the sun disappeared like an eyeball rolling—rooting

Iréne to the spot, turning her to lead, into one of those bewitched and baleful statues of ash in the gardens of Pompeii …

She walked back along the middle of the driveway to the empty hotel. The wind bowled the first dead leaves along in front of her—past the outhouses, their shutters closed, the last tendrils of vine wound round rusty wire beneath the trembling leaves—and all at once the garden took on the colours of winter.

The empty lobby was already quite dark. At this time of day, at this forgotten end of season, in this great body drained of its lifeblood and commotion along with summer, the air—thinner, crystal clear—was full of flimsier, more confused echoes, the slightest sounds doing whatever they wished—a leaf rustling, a wave breaking in the distance, broken down, *resolved* into miraculous slow motion by a succession of diagonal jagged reefs, a gentle breeze through the trees in the garden as persistent as stroking fingers—suddenly attracting unusually close attention to themselves, a morbidly heightened sense of hearing, fleeing the impending silence from moment to moment in exhausting, suffocating intervals like a dying man flees death from one halting breath to the next.

For a long time, not moving, Irène listened to the pounding of the sea which the silence of the lobby brought closer, as if hearing it in a shell. In the gathering darkness the large mirrors drew back into green, undergrowth depths, a fluid space where her silhouette hovered, clear, trapped, plunging with the calm gliding movements of a swimmer. Like in rooms overshadowed by archways of tall trees the darkness seemed to glide down from the ceiling in inky scrolls, water running, continually dissolving, leaving a fine, discrete luminescence on the ground, the parquet floor, on the still-bright gravel of the paths, an unreal moon-softness like those haunting moments during the summer solstice when—although any light in the sky has completely died away, disappeared—the roads and paths stay white far into the night.

Standing in the darkness, one hand resting hesitantly on the wall as if it were stage scenery, motionless, shuddering nervously at the rustling of a branch, the muffled crash of a wave, feeling lethargy, slackening, collapse creeping into her Irène stayed where she was, suspicious of this ominous incarnation, this sudden crack in the tranquil setting—like an animal hears the vague crunching of the hunters' boots around its lair.

But the giddy fever passes. Regaining her stately animal tread, a deadly glint in her eye, Irène goes to switch on the light in her darkened room and, suddenly released, loosed, *determined*, as a swimmer who leaps into the water forgets that a second ago they were able to walk, cold and calculating, a cruel smile on her lips, she begins to write a letter.

"She seemed utterly distraught to me. I found her in tears, completely despairing, only able to keep repeating: 'No, I won't leave, I can't leave!' And her mother arrives tomorrow. How was I to console her? What could I say? That was a painful task you gave me."

Irène and Henri walked back along the beach towards the hotel. The morning was ending crisp and
clear. A long swell of cascading waves pounded noisily
on the shore, more virgin than an ocean atoll—totally
empty.

"What's so frightening about her mother coming to
visit her, that's what I wonder? I've always found her
temperamental, highly strung. Did she by some chance
think this strange holiday wouldn't end? But maybe
you're not too bothered about what happens to her. By
sending me in your place weren't you afraid that coming
from you words of sympathy might ring the tiniest bit
false at the moment?"

Irène stopped and stared at him, hostile, wounded.

"There's something about that insinuation which I
find enormously flattering. But surprising, no. I know
what you're playing at, believe me. For the last month
you've been trying to catch me out, lying in wait for
me. After three months of marriage it's not far short of
appalling. A day hasn't gone by for the past month when
you haven't tried, more patiently than my worst enemy,
to catch me being a hypocrite."

Henri stared at her astounded—her hackles raised,
full of hatred, changed.

"But Irène—you're crazy!"

She looked up sadly.

"Crazy? Come off it. I see it now. I can see it clearly
in your eyes. I've been able to see for days, weeks, that
you despise me."

"Please ... "

"It's absolutely pointless. You see, Henri, I'm not much good at playing ghosts. No doubt that's where the whole trouble starts. Now you've *drawn a distinction* between you and me maybe there's nothing that can be done about it. Don't look so surprised. You understand me perfectly."

Her eyes flashed wildly.

"No, I'm not one of that breed! You're right. No, and I won't ever be! I don't want to be. And if you think— say it then, dare to say it—that I hate them—Christel, Allan, Dolorés, the lot of them—then yes I hate them with all my might, with everything I've got, you're not mistaken—no, don't worry, you're not mistaken."

All of a sudden Henri's eyes glinted oddly.

"You're really quite worked up," he said, icily.

He seemed occupied with some still-obscure line of thought, *rejecting* Irène's violent outburst as the irrelevant tantrum of a spoilt child. He walked on without speaking for a moment.

"Don't you think it's a bit odd, Christel's mother coming?" he said, glaring at her.

Irène paled, then the blood rushed to her cheeks.

"It's me who wrote to her if you must know. I told her what's happening here."

"You did what!" Henri murmured under his breath, white with anger.

"Christel is mad. It's high time her family came and sorted out an episode that's heading nowhere."

He shot her a furious look, contemptuous, unbearable.

"You're such a kind soul."

217

Irène's eyes suddenly filled with tears. She grabbed his hand and looked him up and down, almost timidly.

"Is it you who's talking to me like this, Henri? Really you?"

"How lucky I am to have married a righter of wrongs!"

With a terrible violent gesture he wrenched his hand away from her. Irène burst into tears. Henri stepped back, looked at her with hatred and disgust. Between sobs her voice was humble now, choked.

"Henri … you don't understand … Henri, I was mad … I haven't told you … we're going to have a child … "

"A child … "

Stupefied, he stared at her, at this head hanging down, this face so full of life, burning, blinded with tears—his eyes wide with surprise and fear.

At five o'clock that evening the deserted beach was suddenly woken by the soft sound of an engine; Henri's car came slowly out of the garage. The day was still glorious, warding off winter with the point of a fragile miracle, air so pure it was almost unbreathable. Great luxuriant waves broke on the beach in eruptions of spray, a crested celebration whipped up by jagged, foaming, soaking wings amid pearly iridescence, in astounding, immeasurable, unending solitude.

The car set off slowly along the deserted streets. The wind bowled the first dead leaves, gilded by sun, over the dry tarmac. Above the walls of villas sheltered from strong sea breezes branches rustled gently, soothingly, with the shy sound of a fountain—sometimes meeting in an uneven canopy above the road where the cold, lying in wait, suddenly swooped down to form pools—then abruptly a tangle of dark greenery shut off the avenue, creating a dead end of undergrowth and creeper where the road turned, confused, in the murky light of leaves—trapped by a labyrinth—hemmed in by walls covered in old grey moss, behind them villas plunged in fathomless sleep under archways of greenery—enclosed, turning green, mouldy, listening to their joints creak in the silence like wreckage on the ocean bed. And then the light from the sea burst through again, harrying, fierce, at the end of a dark tunnel.

"What silence!" Henri murmured. The silence reminded him of *the dream*, the dream that had left him devastated when he woke that morning.

He'd found himself with an army on campaign in an ancient castle deep in gloomy Baltic forests. A grey, dignified old building in a horseshoe shape round a paved courtyard, everything green with damp. The mossy roof was rotting beneath constant torrents of rain from the branches: a mournful place and, although there were still leaves on the trees, freezing. And yet around this dismal edifice the usual noisy bustle of an army in the field had for several days taken on a particularly silent, monotonous aspect—behind weakening teams of oxen, wheels slid slowly and noiselessly through the greyish mud of the tracks like ghost-carts, while in the great hall of the castle, faces that grew thinner, more drained of hope day by day pored over plans and maps. From brief glimpses snatched on paths in the woods, from the comings and goings of stealthy couriers, from fearful conversations around the kitchens at nightfall, in the clusters of chilly huts—relentless, obstinate, isolating, elusive, nestling like a swarm of wasps, stubbornly determined to destroy—*bad news* continually filtered through, and every day the faces beneath the helmets got more deathly, every day the tread of the grey insects weighed down by the gruesome, bloated shape of their heavy morion helmets became more wan and grotesque. The presence of the enemy, supple and silent as an octopus, was now finally felt by everyone in the immediate environs of the castle—without any sound giving away their approach except these vague rumours—and, the impending encirclement now ruling out any prospect of escape, in a state of calm despair everyone prepared themselves for the final struggle. From the outset they'd all thought of the *castle* as the central enclave where the last game would be decided.

It was on a misty afternoon, uncannily still, when the branches of the great trees hung down without a murmur over the tall castle gables and into the courtyard, that the *order* came. Immediately in the empty courtyard, half-opening like the hatchways of a three-decker, the two hundred windows of the vast building suddenly sheathed in lightning seemed to fill to bursting, like boxes in a theatre, with muddy helmets, pale implacable faces, fists already clutching rifles and machine guns as if in death, in deafening silence, with the sinister pitching of a stricken vessel on the crest of the wave which goes down flags flying—then all at once the slitted shutters slammed and, lined with black canvas to stop light from showing at night they gave the long façade an air of dismal incarceration, of lame, lopsided mourning like a face with a black silk patch over an empty eye socket. From an upper window, scarring the façade from top to bottom with its magnificent heavy folds, unfurled an enormous black flag.

Heart pounding Henri stood still, alone in eerie silence, overcome by unease in the middle of the empty courtyard, now devastated as if by a whirlwind. A postern gate opened and, unexpectedly prolonging the unreal state of total calm the officer in charge of the final defence came over to him. He was a tall elderly man with a kind noble face framed with long white hair—surprisingly slim and elegant if it hadn't been immediately noticeable that he wasn't in uniform, but wearing black boots, a kind of long, austere mourning dress cut with Protestant severity, a simple white hunting stock round his neck. In one of his ungloved hands he grasped a pistol, barrel raised, but it was quite clear, so meaningful was the position of both hand and weapon, that Henri couldn't help thinking this was less a defensive reaction than for giving the *signal* which, at a stroke, would break the magic silence with a fiendish thunderclap of explosions.

And yet the man walked across as if to ask him—the last idler left in the castle yard, nothing so unlikely in a land destined for fire and brimstone than someone strolling about in the middle of an artillery bombardment—to leave what in a few minutes would become a place of terror. And as he closed the postern gate behind him, cast out the last trace of humanity from this realm of darkness, separated him from what was going to happen *there*, he offered him his hand. But the hand was raised as if bearing the flaming two-edged sword of the archangel, the gate slammed shut with a dull crash, and the magic circle closed forever on the forbidden kingdom.

Since that morning the dream had lurked inside his head like a bee in a closed room, banging itself against the window—one of those haunting dreams, linked like scenes in a play, which despite their obscurity still have enormous power to *illustrate*—one of those dreams that makes whole days fade away, setting your mind adrift in a peculiar permeable world, its watertightness suspect— with one of those fault lines running through its thickest part, one of those *flaws* you see in diamonds but daren't stick your nail into.

"Yes, this evening—this very evening ... "

The last villas left behind, bitter grass from the nearby dunes already swallowing their little gardens through the thin wire fences, the car went faster now. For as far as the eye could see the road cut through a drab ashen landscape where even the sunlight was sad, cooled here and there by the moon-like touch of a patch of sand. Against the light of late evening the horizon of the sea vanished into the rising mist. Not even a house now. No one. All of a sudden one of those gentle flurries of cold wind that come at the start of late autumn evenings leapt up unexpectedly, crossed the road at a gallop like a frightened animal breaking cover—the smooth sand of the road rippled like folds of fabric, pale grass plunged over the edge of the embankment. In the distance the waves, so clear, so green, were covered with opaque grey film.

"At this moment Irène is dressing for dinner ... Allan is on his way back to the hotel from the beach ... " With incredible clarity he pictured the tall figure wandering alone on the naked beach, captured at that unusual angle where in certain films, seen from behind with the camera almost at ground level, the hero walks away down a road, an empty shore, each step seeming to draw a tight web of gossamer towards the horizon and, getting further and further away, to empty the landscape like a room stripped of furniture, suddenly giving the houses, the flowers, the garden gates an air of blind nakedness, floating anxiety, abandonment.

Now he saw the places laid in the great, cold, empty dining room, where for the last few days everyone had had all their meals together at the same table. Facing a sea that was now always grey, in the evening the room drew back into a nobler formality, a state of expectation. The immaculate tablecloth, the dramatic array of cut glass, heavy silver in the middle of the vast room, its corners filled with darkness, suddenly reminded him obscurely of some Last Supper, a sacred meal, whether for a funeral or to please the gods. Stood stiffly in their double ranks the leather chairs, one of which would be unoccupied tonight. Faces suddenly filled the shadows in this tall dark room, fugitive, intangible—eyes avoiding each other, saying nothing, a hand searching for the reassurance of another hand—dense and dark the wine flowed into a glass that a ceremonious, ironic hand slowly raised.

"This very evening ... "

The blood throbbed dully in his temples. In the chill of evening a shudder ran through him, persistent, electrifying.

"It's a touch of fever," he thought. "I'm feverish. Bah! So what!"

The car was now surging along a smooth wide road that ran along the top of the cliffs. In the gathering darkness white bouquets of ghosts sometimes rose towards the car like puffs of steam, spurting out of a hollow of black rock: those beautiful feathery storm geysers that angels create for men in that *slow motion* peculiar to hypnotizers. Far out to sea, across its already-dark surface, a lighthouse lit up—and evening suddenly turned to night.

"What a lost coastline!" thought Henri, in the grip of vague uneasiness. The pointed waves leapt up unhurriedly, playful, languid, with barely a noise, just for fun, to relax after a good day, like elves caught dancing in the moonlight by someone out for a walk.

Opposite the now darkened sea, just inland, a faint, hazy pearly glow that seemed to hover just above the ground, *placed* there like dew, was stirring on the mown lawns—another last reflection of day, and yet already—with quiet resonance, as if coming to life at the height of summer on warm roads like a swathe of pale flower sepals opening—already moonlight.

"It's time for dinner now." From a distance the evening at the hotel unfolded before him in its remorseless sequence, the baleful ceremonial of a funeral ballet, the motionless haste of the last act of a tragedy. Coming into the dark hall that suddenly lights up—familiar gestures like garlands round the table—the lone hotel shining out from every window, facing a sea that was dark all the way to the horizon.

He stopped on the side of the road and walked along the top of the cliff, slowly, hesitantly. After the intoxicating speed of the last few minutes the ground beneath his unsteady feet seemed soft and spongy. Without the headlamps the darkness was almost total. Dull thunder punctuated by silence rose periodically from the unseen sea at the foot of the cliffs. Inland the moon shone mysteriously over tranquil open spaces, bare fields overwhelmed by the magic of the night.

He sat on the edge of the cliff and, legs dangling, stared vaguely out to sea. Inertia rose from this abyss, fascinated him. Freezing hands gripping the rock, legs turned to jelly, he felt his head fill with whirling darkness, cold gusts of wind. His heart beat fitfully. He closed his eyes. Long minutes passed in vertigo, a delirium he gave in to, invited.

He opened his eyes on brilliant moonlight, on what was now total night. A mysterious stillness stretched out over the almost motionless sea. A little way inland a dog barked, so comforting, so calm. A cold breeze blew from off the land. Briskly he shook himself and set off in the car again.

Hours went by, dull, unvarying. Occasionally the car left the main road, drove through lonely woods where on tight corners pale tree trunks flashed past in the headlight beams, surreal as the spokes of a fairground wheel. A low squat roof could sometimes be made out near the roadside, flattened like an animal's night-time den. The engine purred steadily, softly, drowsy and cautious as if wrapped in cotton wool. Now and again a bluish mist rolled over the hedges. Then the dense, quilted country night came out to get some fresh air, flapped like an unbuttoned coat, and the road sent him back towards the horizon out to sea. He drove on, obeying the monotony of speed, the muffled motion. A faint blue-green light washed up from the instruments on the dashboard, lighting up his face, and sometimes his reflection appeared on the windscreen, a colourless patch, barely alive, having a tête-à-tête with him, a dubious intimacy, jaws silver with light, eyes flooded with impenetrable darkness, vaguely bizarre—more solemn—other.

Through the gathering mist he saw the lights of a harbour. Along the grassy roadside houses loomed up bright white in the headlights, then the car plunged down a narrowing street and suddenly his way was blocked at the edge of lapping water in the hazy light of neon signs. Distinct, making a surprising ringing noise on the cobblestones, occasional footsteps walked along the pavement of the little square. With a muffled leap a cat ran in front of the car. For a second or two Henri was in a daze—he thought he'd suddenly woken confused from a blurred dream, in a strange town, and opened his bedroom shutters, still unsure whether these scarce faltering footsteps, this cold wind were the forerunners of dawn or the last comings and goings of evening.

Suddenly he was frozen, his teeth chattered. He went into a bar and collapsed onto a seat, dazed by the harsh lights, the unpleasant warmth as if he'd been punched. A morose old woman was knitting behind the empty counter, face expressionless.

The long seedy room was deserted. A relay switch clunked and the inner room was promptly plunged in darkness. Instinctively Henri's eyes scoured this suddenly secret shadow-light where bottles and glasses glinted faintly. Half-lying on the seat, her mournful inanimate face mesmerized him like a judge's. "How can I ask her where I am? *It'll be the end of me*," he repeated to himself, stupidly.

Still knitting the woman got up, and without taking her eyes off her work came over to him. Immediately an icy hand clung to every inch of him, the table lunged up towards him—he passed out.

"You're still such a child! It's almost as if you were frightened."

Transfixed, self-conscious, suddenly feeling close to tears, Jacques undressed awkwardly. Irène's large fragrant room, cluttered with heavy, harshly-coloured fabrics intimidated him. The only light was from a dimmed lamp in one corner: the faint almost horizontal glow gave the large bed, its glazed pink counterpane shimmering like a beach in the darkness, a presence which made him uncomfortable.

Near him, under her bathrobe, he could feel the freshness, the faint scent of her body that had just come from the bath, and he kissed her bare arm shyly, tenderly, as if it were a mother's.

"A little child … " Irène repeated, touched, taking his head between her hands and raising it out of the shadows towards her.

"You're sure Henri won't come back?"

Irène's voice sounded thoughtful, serious, as if cracking from some vague anxiety.

"No, don't worry. He won't come back tonight."

She seemed to shake off a troublesome thought. Jacques shuddered distractedly.

"Put that dressing gown on. The white one, it suits you. It's chilly tonight you know … You look nice like that," she added with an affectionate, engaging smile—and putting her arms round his neck she stared at him.

Silence returned to prowl the room again. Ill at ease, Jacques glanced up at the ceiling where a moth threw long, flitting shadows. Outside the fabric-lined windows of the conjugal bedroom they heard the wind rummaging. Two or three times, at irregular intervals, a pile-driver of waves echoed dully nearby like someone knocking on a door in the dead of night.

"The hotel's got rather gloomy don't you think?"

"Don't be nervous. Give me your hand … you're here!" Irène went on, leaning closer to his face, staring at him greedily.

In his mind Jacques saw the long icy corridors of the deserted hotel in their dim light—like a mineshaft at night, the creaking gangways of an ocean liner where a night porter wanders up and down, beset by deep yawns. This oasis of low light that silently half-opened for him like a sanctuary—surrounded by empty rooms, lost inside this echoing shell that made you lower your voice.

"Allan was strange at dinner this evening. Didn't you notice?"

Irène got up, irritated, and quickly checked the windows were shut.

"Leave Allan out of it, please. Do you want to spoil tonight—our night? Maybe our only one."

"Being so preoccupied—he's not usually like that. Yes, there's something worrying him, I'm sure of it. And Christel was pretty peculiar too. Did you see the way she stared at him when he got up to say goodbye to her? It wasn't a natural sort of look, I tell you."

"Listen!"

Stiffening, breathless, Irène cut him off with an imperious gesture. In the corridor on the other side of the thin partition a door was rattling slightly, uncertainly. Holding their breath, for long seconds they listened to the dark silence.

"It's the wind," Jacques went on, slightly pale. "There's always a window open in the corridor."

"It's *his* room … " A note of alarming *conviction* suddenly came into Irène's voice, as if she'd had difficulty convincing herself.

Jacques kissed her gently, her lips suddenly helpless, unprotected, burning.

"See, you're nervous as well … "

"Hold me."

She was shivering now. Faced with a vulnerable, defeated Irène Jacques's shyness evaporated. He held her

229

tightly, kissed her hard. Her beautiful moist eyes, slightly scared, so close to his, kept on staring. Softly she began moaning.

"Come on," she murmured, teeth chattering, voice hurrying, brisk …

When he woke, still half-asleep, it seemed the room was suddenly very dark. He had that same slight feeling of uneasiness you get when you wake up late after a bad night, in that deceptive darkness of closed shutters which, slipping through chinks in the curtains, filtering through every seam, morning's pale fingers are already contradicting. Yet in the corner the lamp was glowing softly. It was as if the room was being crushed beneath the heavy fabrics, their great black folds. Over it hung the atmosphere of an unhappy vigil. More than anything he was surprised by the long curtains in the alcove, rippling like the sides of a tent, rather worrying—behind which the walls seemed to shrink back, abandon this dismal, mediocre bed, this separate and forbidden sleep.

"I was asleep!" he thought strangely, feeling a pang of remorse as if he'd abandoned some heroic vigil—let *time* slip by, as if bewitched by the mournful lethargy of Gethsemane.

An obscure toneless dream had taken possession of this lofty room, gradually bestriding the tousled bodies, hiding its face in higher contemplation, shrouded in a mesmerizing, obsessive immobility that froze these dark curtains as if in ice, the pale patches of clothes collapsed stiffly like piles of rocks under the sudden force of gravity.

Heart heavy as if from nausea he let his gaze drift over the griffins, the pale flowers on the tapestry. The sound of the waves was more muffled now. "The tide's going out," he said to himself stupidly, at a loss for any other thoughts. Beyond unseen walls his mind pierced the silence of dark rooms, a silence like a fast-flowing torrent, smooth, all-consuming. A door rattled in the corridor again, faltering, slow.

He turned to Irène. Sitting up beside him, motionless as marble, eyes wide in the darkness, face furrowed with obsessive concentration she pricked up her ears—now suddenly the other side of an abyss, cut off by a great distance, like those grim *hoaxes* that dreams play where you wake up cheerfully to find a stone statue beside you.

"What's wrong?"

Sitting up quickly he grabbed her by both hands, as if overpowering a madwoman. Her face fell again, retreated feebly into shadow. Suddenly Jacques tore away the veil, broke through the curse of this night of pretence, feeling violence well up in him, a fit of rage.

"Why did you get me to come here?"

Her voice was hushed, trembling, swept away by gusts of choking terror.

"I'm frightened."

Sitting at the table, motionless in the middle of the completely darkened room, Allan looked out the open windows at the great squares of sky filled with glittering stars in front of him, which the full moon shrouded with a faint blue haze like a sheet—like that incense of light that rises over capital cities at night, or steam from the flanks of a hot, exhausted animal. Peaceful moonlight came through the window on the garden side, cast a great black cross on the bed. Suddenly the trees nearby seemed to rustle of their own accord, with a single, solemn impulse. Great domes of silver light, velvety, breastplated, rose into the sacred night in dreamlike tiers, incensed with blue sacrificial smoke, pierced to the depths of their dark greenness with mysterious caves like gaps in the clouds. Occasionally a leaf fluttered down, a mere little ghost, frightened by this heavy rapture.

Beyond the beach a liquid blue heavenly snow came down the hills to gather in the valleys, flakes rolling gently as clouds, becoming lakes, giving the impression of lethargic heaviness, defeat, drowsiness.

"Let yourself go," he thought. "Yes, it's all so easy. Sink ... '*refuse*', as they say about a horse that shies at a fence. Is that the last word? ... "

He uncapped a tiny flask and poured a few drops of black liquid into a glass of water. As he stirred it the spoon made a reassuring silvery sound against the sides—closing the circle of gentle routine round his wrist like a trap.

"Coffee ... a bad cup of coffee ... "

Slowly he went over to the window and leant out towards the trees in the garden. Long, luxuriant, rippling shadows, deep as ink, lay across the lawn; while a few feet away from these patches, as unsettling as sleeping pools, the light turned into a chirping song, vapour, the quiet reverberation of a million insects hopping on the ground—a rejoicing, dancing deliverance, release. The grey light wiped any sign of life from his motionless figure, froze it, cleansed it of all *particularity*, absorbed it into the silent unseeing façade, into these magic gardens caught unawares by some deft work of sorcery. "The guest made of stone,"[9] he thought to himself, bitterly.

He turned back to the darkened room. A moonbeam slipped across the glowing parquet floor like a piece of silk. Somewhere in the darkness a clock ticked away the seconds. The extraordinary stillness of the moon sucked the life out of this dark sombre room through the windows, as an embalmer drains a skull through the nostrils, replacing the warm breath of life with pure icy ether—effortlessly merging the empty room with the dark grottos of the enchanted garden. Part of a poem he wrote when he was young suddenly came back from deep down in his memory: '*If I rise and walk beside this sleeping woman, with her lolling tongue, those trance-like gestures that betray me, I will search reluctantly for the painful wound in my side which turns me so pale—whose spilt blood makes this unhappy room as cold as death.*'

The moon rummaged through the room as if it were a forgotten attic, salvaging a unique, suddenly *important* detail here and there, throbbing with the same subdued life as an arm, a hand shooting out from under a landslide, a car crash. As dramatic as a spotlight the moon picked out the shimmering table, a jumble of scattered papers. Allan's elastic stride roamed the room. Outside, the magical blue shower was still falling in great soft waves, lulling the garden to sleep like snow.

He sat at the table again, glanced distractedly through some papers. A slight breeze swept through the room, the sheets of paper blew in the air, dancing. He swung round: silent as a shadow, Christel had just come in.

For a few moments they looked at each other, not moving—him a dark shape against the brilliance of the moon, back arched, face alert—her, hands lost in a long white bathrobe, leaning against the closed door, blocking any escape, head lowered, the fierce pose of the hunted woman.

"It's you, Christel," he said eventually in a low, mistrustful voice.

"Yes." The voice was blank, barely breathing.

"What's the matter? Come in, sit down. Would you like me to turn on the light?"

"No." Still the same murmur, the same low voice, *subordinate*, with barely a timbre.

The white form moved forward, floated slowly towards the table. The bare humble feet were suddenly caught in a moonbeam. The pallid face crouched beneath the heavy dark hair like a crime in the depths of a darkened house. Suddenly uneasy at these wandering, hovering, sleepwalker steps he stopped her, unmasked her in a harsh voice.

"What have you come here for?"

Her despair burst out in a hiss.

"You're going to die … "

In a sudden fit of anger he sat up facing her.

"What do you mean by that?"

"You're going to die. You want to die, I know it. I've known for days, weeks."

234

He took her hands, calmed her.

"Christel, what a crazy notion."

Her voice rose, harder, more confident.

"No, don't talk to me like a child. Please, I've guessed everything."

He could feel this voice tumbling down inside him, corrosive, grim, heavy with unexpected knowledge, with serious, shrewd clairvoyance—peaceful, already beyond tears. Surprised, he looked up at her face: pale but almost smiling. She was very beautiful.

"It's true, Christel. This is my last night."

Her face set hard, bleeding from an open wound. Like a gentle downward slope to complicity this suffering affection, this silence, led Allan to make admissions.

"I knew it. When you arrived … "

"Yes, everything was already decided. And before these last long weeks I'd never have never believed just how much of a liability death is, even when it's packed away inside a suitcase, how scandalous, difficult to hide."

He suppressed a wild laugh.

"Don't laugh. Your laugh hurts me."

Quickly, sharply, eyes suddenly half-closed he searched the dishevelled hair, the scant attire, bare feet, the offered body. Brazenly he looked up at her and put his hand on her bare arm.

"Have you come to *save* me?" he hissed, maliciously.

"A virgin for the last love. Quite a role for you isn't it—and how heroic!"

He gripped her arm roughly, his face close to hers.

"I could take advantage of that, you know. Perhaps it still appeals."

"Here I am." Fierce pride blazed in her trembling voice. The words stuck in Allan's throat; Christel promptly untied her robe. Face against hers he put his hand out and stopped her, distraught.

"You've got courage, Christel. Forgive me!"

Suddenly haggard, defeated, choked with tenderness, he clasped her warm heroic flesh to him, soft as spring rain—covered the unblinking eyes with kisses, rubbed the stubborn, tear-streaked, happy head against his chest with blind affection.

"My poor love, how brave you are! So you really love me so much?"

She pushed her head against his chest over and over again, moaning, her sobs coming quicker, overlapping like bubbles on boiling water.

"Oh yes! … If only you knew … "

She kissed his hands gently, humbly, wetting them with tears.

"You're not going to die, tell me … You won't ever leave me … "

He freed his hands, kissed her forehead and took her to the window. He gazed long and hard at the garden, which was swooning almost shamelessly in the moonlight, the melting, adoring night. She watched him, mesmerized.

"I've left you all already," he said sadly, without looking round.

"Left … ?"

"I gave my word … "

"To Dolorés?"

Anguish rose quickly in her voice.

"Yes. We're going to die together. To see tomorrow would only dishonour me."

"Is it so important, Allan?" She stared up at him, imploring, serious. He touched her hair gently and looked at her, suddenly solemn.

"Perhaps. Oh, I know the scorn it can attract to carry out a resolution! Tonight more than anyone. How much our motives are pushed aside, dispelled during the course of our life, even the shortest periods of time; a day, a week, as long as you agree to go on living. I know I won't die tonight the same man who arrived here two months ago. Two months already. Not the same, nor for the same reasons. Can I even know *who* I'll be when I die in two hours time? What point is there chasing after fleeting shadows?" he added with a weary gesture. "And yet, Christel, the resolution is made."

"So why did you come here, hurt us, make us all unhappy?"

"Yes, it's true, I've been playing. I've played with all of you, like you put on a sheet at night and pretend to be a ghost. An unhappy demon … and besides … I don't know … everything was confused. I was living from day to day, in a frenzy, trying to beat chance at its own clever game. If now—tonight—I can forgive myself for this black prank it's because I can tell myself that deep down I've always known I'm prepared to pay the price."

A perverse gentleness, a dangerous state of abandon drove him to betray confidences, jeopardize himself.

237

When he continued his voice was low, broken by a shudder of fear.

"And you see Christel, I know a secret now. A terrible secret. Yes, I know that at the time of a man's death—when he doesn't have his throat cut quickly, unexpectedly, when it's a *violent* death, when it lets you *see it coming*—there'll always be a crowd round him. You only have to look at theatres, executions. But what I didn't realize is that it isn't *good* to let death go wandering around openly in this world. I didn't realize ... it disturbs, awakens the death that sleeps deep down inside people, like a child in a woman's belly. Like when a woman meets a pregnant woman—even if she looks away—yes, deep down inside them, if you were to go there, you'd feel they were *accomplices* ... "

He looked at her, gave a nod of childish conviction.

" ... Yes, all of a sudden it's their own death that's moving inside them. And it's not easy to find yourself *up against* it."

"Don't say such things. It's not possible. You're driving me mad," she told him, angrily. Although still so close she sensed he was reaching a secret exit already, escaping from this unsealed room, becoming part of the night, dissolving into it.

He reacted harshly.

"Ask Gérard then. He knows too. He's guessed a lot of things."

She clung to his shoulders with both hands and looked up at him in utter despair.

"Why do you want to die?"

"Oh! That's a long story ... "

He shrugged wearily.

"Why I wanted to die probably isn't of much importance anymore. What's the point? But I'll turn your question round. Do you really think I could live *now?*"

He shook with sudden, bitter laughter.

"Saved from a watery grave, having netted a beautiful woman into the bargain. Yes, I could probably go on living—provided I didn't die of ridicule.

"Do you know why people never forgive a failed suicide, a faked suicide? They're taking *revenge*. It's the donkey kicking the beaten hero, the *supporter* booing the unlucky champion. High hopes dashed, the need for excitement thwarted—they soon go sour, suddenly change into black humour."

He turned towards the window and continued his dreamy soliloquy in a hushed voice.

"Yes, when I came here with Dolorés I thought I was free, leaning on her by my own choice. And if I die tonight it's almost—mostly—because everyone's conspiring in my death, chasing me away, driving me to a heroic *exit*."

She stood there in front of him, hard, wounded, wounding.

"You're pretty arrogant … "

He smiled with unhappy pride.

"Yes, there's that. And also … it's so difficult to say … "

His voice dropped, suddenly settled on an innermost thought.

" … deeper than anything, perhaps—yes, it must have withstood more than anything … I don't know … the founders of religions in certain obscure situations—when you raise certain of people's expectations: a mysterious requirement to achieve, to not let things *slip*—to lift the gaze of the faithful forever; to be consumed in their eternally famished mouths, a fiery, everlasting food … "

He stared at Christel with strange intensity, the pale face that was filling with vague dread. She looked up at him, a humble prayer.

"And me, Allan! … "

"You!"

In a moment of great, confused emotion he covered her hands with loving kisses.

"For you too. For you especially. For keeping your dignity … "

She gazed into the darkest depths of his eyes, drank long and deep of the panic, the dizzy fever that was there.

"I'll love you forever, saved, lost … wherever you take me—yes, whatever … your plaything, your slave—even if it means I'm destroyed, even if I can't do anything for you."

His eyes were adrift, floating over her, distraught, crucified by a lucid thought.

"Yes, you love me, Christel. But I've confused everything. You love me, but only mingled with my death."

She stiffened in violent rage.

"You're insane!"

"I made a pact. What could I ever be to you, *saved?* When you've loved me dazzlingly dressed, hidden beneath my mantle of blood—mingled with it like a king in his purple robes … "

He held up his hand, imposed silence, his strange voice surrounding, caressing a secret certainty—becoming louder again, disappearing, dissolving into the night, his accomplice.

"I'm losing you, but I'll always be with you."

"So you think I can still live once you're dead?"

"Yes I do. The hand that wounds can also heal. There's great power in scandal when it's over. There's always great virtue in achievement. And at least *this* will have been, and there'll be nothing left to say. There's a sublime purifying force in what's *done*. You'll see how you'll be released, lightened—how everything will be put in order. You'll see how good, how much better life will be Christel, when I'm dead."

"Why are you tormenting me?"

But she wasn't struggling anymore, she let herself go, roll away, left tears behind, bound hand and foot by his devastating words. One last storm blew up in Allan's mind: wrung by frenzied fingers his thoughts explored every possibility—now beyond living he tried to make the hour of reckoning blaze like a torch, explode. Suddenly he went across to the table.

"Look!"

The naked voice made her shudder. In the middle of the pool of brilliant moonlight, with enthralling solemnness he picked up the glass of poison. Slowly she came closer, mesmerized, staring. Seconds went by. Christel's hand, her arm began to shake uncontrollably, involuntarily. He could tell she was battling with an overpowering temptation. A wild glint came into his eyes—a flash of triumph, acute envy.

He put the glass down some way away from her.

241

"Now you can *see* what you've never stopped looking at."

Her constant trembling made her quiver against him like a bowstring. He put his hand on her shoulder. Suddenly awake she opened her eyes, distraught with grief, sunk her nails into him as if she were drowning. He kissed her lips, soft and warm with tears, and then gently, firmly, one after the other, moved her hands away.

"May everything I love be taken from me. And now Christel, goodbye. It's over—leave me."

He closed the door firmly, lit a cigarette. He was breathing heavily, with difficulty. The peaceful sound of the rising tide came in through the windows. For as far as the eye could see the trees in the garden were frosted with the light of the full moon. In the depths of the dark room the clock ticked away the familiar seconds.

Then he heard the door open again, and, calmly, at the far end of the room, he saw his last moment come.

TRANSLATOR'S NOTES

1 p 65 *hoi polloi* Here Gracq uses the Turkish word *râya*, a term of contempt for Infidel subjects of the Ottoman Empire.

2 p 122 *les Trois Glorieuses* Reference to the three-day July revolution of 1830.

3 p 127 *Fête de la Fédération* Celebration of the first anniversary of the storming of the Bastille held on 14th July 1790 on the Champs-de-Mars and attended by Louis XVI. It took place only once more, in 1792. In 1880 it became the French national festival.

4 p 148 *O! Swear ... tops* Here Gracq inverts the order of Shakespeare's lines.

5 p 152 *communicating vessels* In the original: '*vases communicants*'—the title of a book by André Breton.

6 p 159 *jotted ... griffin* There is an untranslatable play on words here. Gracq uses the verb *griffoner* (to jot or scribble) and the noun *griffon*, or griffin.

7 p 188 *rallied round ... plume* Allusion to a remark Henri IV is said to have made before the Battle of Ivry—"*Rally round my white plume. You'll always see it on the road to honour and victory*".

8 p 192 *happy few* In English in the original text.

9 p 228 *The guest made of stone* Reference to the ghost of the Commendatore in the legend of *Don Juan*.

TRANSLATOR'S AFTERWORD

A dark stranger … *Un beau ténébreux* … the very title of Julien Gracq's second novel symbolizes the complexity and startling obliqueness of a book that, on its publication in 1945, was described by Edmond Jaloux, writing in Psyché, as 'a black diamond' whose dark brilliance set it apart from the literature of its time.

Who is this stranger? The answer lies partly in the Romantic tradition. In the influential French translation of *Amadis de Gaula*, Garcia Rodrigues Montalvo's sixteenth-century tale of chivalry, the eponymous hero refers to himself as the '*Beau ténébreux*'. By placing his central character, the repellent and equivocally chivalrous Allan Murchison in a long line of Romantic heroes, Gracq links the narrative with four centuries of literature. But by using the indefinite article—A *Dark Stranger*—he strips him of uniqueness. So from the outset both novel and hero are put in context.

Gracq got the idea for the book while a prisoner of war in a camp near Hoyerswerda in what was then German Silesia. It was inspired by an obscure poem of Vigny's, *Les amants de Montmorency* in which two lovers make a suicide pact. In *Carnets du grand chemin* he describes how he wrote it in bed in the prison hut, not just for lack of a table; they were so ill-fed they only got up for a few hours a day so as to save energy. It was his job to divide up the daily ration of black bread. Never had the Lord's Prayer—'give us this day our daily bread'—seemed so relevant.

A Dark Stranger is the product of this period of captivity, its ascetic routines. Arresting, prescient, it rises from the forest plains of Silesia only to be transposed onto the thundering tides of Brittany. Much influenced by Ernst Jünger and German Romantic literature, Gracq sets the story in another place where poetic traditions are strong. It resembles both the wild Breton coastline and the Silesian plain: sombre, unceasing, moving in cool sensual waves, sometimes calm, always unsettling.

Hence the inter-war setting assumes particular significance. The 1920s were a time of insouciance, conspicuous wealth; the jazz age epitomized by F Scott Fitzgerald. But in *A Dark Stranger*—as for Fitzgerald in other ways—the period has something of a lament. Its wealthy, neurotic characters seem to be in mourning: but is this for the past horrors of 1914-18—which perhaps significantly are never mentioned—or for those to come in 1939-45, and which, so real and immediate for the author, haunt the Hôtel des Vagues in much the same way as Allan Murchison, the spectre of approaching death in his bloodstained robes? It is as if France is about to hurl itself into the abyss with him.

Critics often divide Gracq's novels into the 'surreal'— *Au Château d'Argol* and *Le rivage des syrtes*—and the more 'realistic'—*Un beau ténébreux* and *Un balcon en forêt*. Yet the apparent suspensions of time that reoccur in the book show such categories to be as simplistic as classing Gracq as a Surrealist.

The era is nonetheless determined by the tone: the then-fashionable anglophilia is also found in François Mauriac's novels; the in-crowd at the hotel is known as '*la bande* straight': Allan's glamorous Anglo-French parentage (Gregory, too, is apparently 'Scottish'), his quotes from Wilde, his cantish schoolboy affectations, the monocle, Eton bow ties and English suits—a style once popular with pupils at the Lycée Henri IV, including the young Julien Gracq, who in a spirit of self-mockery maintained it as a student.

Englishness plays a particular role in the novel, one that operates on several levels. Allan's parentage gives him cachet, explains his icy, derisive elegance, perhaps even his supposed superiority over his hot-blooded Latin acolytes. Yet the situation is not without irony. Although the other characters fall short of the ideal he sets, it is their failings that ultimately put them on a higher level than him; something they, even he, perhaps realize but are unwilling to admit.

Gracq also seems to have had Anglo-Saxon leanings— not least his reserve. Yet his brand of anglophilia is atypical. He admired English coolness while recognizing that its emotional detachment is often accompanied by a lack of intellectual acuity. Widely read in English literature, he first visited the country in 1929. His observations, not published until 1992, draw interesting comparisons. He disliked the cynicism, the destructive criticism prevalent in France after 1918, admiring the British for still having

'Victorian values'—something that would stand them in good stead in 1940. He felt this was what accounted for the very different national responses to the outbreak of war. But after a visit in the 1990s he felt the English had become 'more like the French … '

In *A Dark Stranger* such lucid details are occasionally blurred. In some respects the 1920s it portrays resembles post-war France, the *Trente Glorieuses* of socio-economic recovery and collective memory loss, as if Gracq is foretelling future events. Drawing from the author's experience, Gérard refers to his time as a prisoner at Hoyerswerda. Unless this is intended as a memory of 1914-18, it might imply he is writing his diary after World War II—which is clearly not the case. Such manipulations of time are a reminder of Gracq's more overtly surreal work, as well as Jünger's *Auf den Marmorklippen*,[1] which so influenced his writing.

Other personal memories also contribute to this sense of shifting eras. The group that gravitates around Allan exists in a climate of approaching apocalypse more reminiscent of the period immediately prior to the war than of the jazz age. Years later Gracq described the threat of civil war that existed in France between 1933-36 (far more real than in 1968). Witnessing the Spanish Civil War and German aggression, his generation had a sense of impending disaster. An atmosphere, he said, 'to which one couldn't be indifferent'.

With Allan and Dolorés's arrival comes a world-weariness that stifles every conversation, every pleasure.

1 *On the Marble Cliffs*

'Civil war' is a not inaccurate description of the situation that exists from then on: the Allan faction versus the rest.

So who is Allan? This question, which Christel finally asks Gérard, frames the whole novel. Yet the little we know about him—despite or perhaps because of Gregory's reminiscences in his letter to Gérard—is ambivalent. As Gérard tells Henri, our conjectures are diverted by the obliqueness of the Devil.

Oddly Allan, with his plan for a rational suicide, seems more of an Existential than a Surrealist hero. Acutely conscious of himself, almost stereotypically 'masculine', everything he says and does reinforces a self-image he has crafted since childhood. His Anglo-French upbringing seems to give him the least endearing characteristics of both nations; nations that are essentially very similar despite surface differences. One critic described him as the ideal of every troubled adolescent boy: influenced by German Romanticism, with an incomplete knowledge of Gide and Montherlant, whose aim is to be irresistible to women, intriguing to men, to collect rare works of art, ravage hearts and minds alike, then die beautifully by their own hand. In his final conversation with Gérard, Allan admits as much—if he ever admits anything.

Yet this is too superficial a judgement for a writer as subtle as Gracq. What he creates with incisive irony is a modern figure, one familiar to us. Allan is godless, supremely logical, preoccupied with the impression he makes. Materially successful, a chess-problem solver par excellence, for him people are as interesting as the treasures he collects—no more, no less. While protecting

249

his privacy, beneath the mask—the 'permanent look of Werther' as Irène describes it—his aim is to provoke reaction. In Gregory's words he 'burns life at both ends' according to his own existential code of perfection. Then, like the meteor Christel sees from the train, he makes a spectacular exit, destroys the self he has created, believing in it to the last. In his book on Gracq, Hubert Haddad said of Allan: "What is Byron doing at the seaside?"[2]

Gracq's message might be, 'don't live your life like this'. Allan's gifts are squandered in a quest for an ideal that has no more substance than his reflection in the mirror. Ultimately he is a study in failure.

For different and often contradictory motives the others encourage Allan in his quest. Irène's denouncement at Roscaër spurs him on to self-gratification, not self-knowledge. Part of their milieu, even its avatar, he stretches its boundaries until neither it nor he can return to their former dimensions. He creates a void around himself into which the rest feel themselves falling. In an attempt to stop their world disintegrating they cling to the familiar—literature, philosophy, music. But like a character in one of their favourite operas, Allan has knocked away the corner stone, leaving them adrift in an intellectual vacuum.

What of sexuality? Gracq was a private man; his interest lay in the spiritual and intellectual cross-currents that create or destroy relationships. Sexual desire is a force that should be balanced philosophically. Nowhere is this clearer than in Allan's relationship with Christel, where to the end the

2 *Julien Gracq. La forme d'une vie.* Le Castor astral 1986

carnal is kept in check. Irène's contempt for him seems to stem from the fact that he does *not* seduce Christel, at least physically—behaviour that is beyond her grasp.

While acknowledging the role of personal experience in his work, Gracq gives more weight to imagination, the realm of visions. Hence the visible world becomes a 'bearer of keys'. Hence the unreal fascination that Allan exercises, the almost divine attributes of Christel and Dolorés. As desirable as Irène may be, she is trapped in a body, envious of those who are not. Sexuality is incidental, refreshingly so. Perhaps there are traces of misogyny, a tendency to portray women as harpies or beauties from the age of chivalry; or as visions.

This is not the place to discuss Gracq's relationship with the Surrealist movement, which is examined in detail elsewhere. Although close to André Breton, he never belonged to his group. It is nonetheless worth noting that his study of Breton appeared just a few years after *A Dark Stranger*.

It is thus unsurprising that Allan owes something to Breton: the focus of a personality cult, he seems to hold the key to some central mystery. For him death is simply a stage in our ongoing life, a view once expressed by Breton when he said: 'I want to be taken to the cemetery in a removal van'.

Yet Allan's role never ceases to be oblique. At times he seems to be playing a vast game of chess, not only with the other characters but with the literary and Surrealist themes which, through him, exert their influence on the narrative: Poe, Rimbaud, keywords, magnetic fields, vanishing points, planetary orbits. For others—although the shift in roles is barely perceptible—he acts as a form of external siphon that feeds a series of communicating vessels, an image used by Gérard in his diary. This, the interrelation of our waking and dreaming lives, how they cross-fertilize, is arguably the book's predominant Surrealist element, one that draws on Breton's work *Les vases communicants*.[3] The part played by dreams is substantial yet understated; it is often hard to distinguish dream from reality. And although none of the characters dream about Allan specifically, it is apparent that he inspires, even dictates, the content of their dreams. He inhabits both worlds, blurring the already porous boundary between them.

To French and English readers alike, Gracq's work can seem impenetrable. Yet in a world where communication is becoming homogeneous, the clarity of his language is a reminder of the purifying power of the word; that it can reveal without blinding. In an interview with Gracq in 1986, Jean Carrière commented that his work sometimes gives the impression of being translated from another language. Gracq replied that, on the contrary, his (unfulfillable) wish was that it should remain so close to its French roots as to be 'untranslatable'.

Gracq's avoidance of the literary scene—he refused the Prix Goncourt in 1951—seems more justified than ever today, when the self-promotion encouraged by publishers and authors alike has such a corrosive effect on the integrity of literature. The work of many contemporary

3 *Communicating Vessels.*

writers is obscured by their public profile. Gracq, by contrast, effaces himself. It is his work that shines, not him. When he died in 2007 at the age of ninety-seven, one of the few to be published in the Pléiade in his lifetime, the press described his passing as 'discreet'. It is perhaps the most fitting tribute for an author.

Michel Tournier, the well-known French novelist, once spoke about influences on his own work. Prominent among them was Julien Gracq. When asked to elaborate he had only this to say: "Gracq ... read all of him".

CHRISTOPHER MONCRIEFF
Harz Mountains
September 2008

Pushkin Press

Pushkin Press was founded in 1997. Having first rediscovered European classics of the twentieth century, Pushkin now publishes novels, essays, memoirs, children's books, and everything from timeless classics to the urgent and contemporary.

This book is part of the Pushkin Collection of paperbacks, designed to be as satisfying as possible to hold and to enjoy. It is typeset in Monotype Baskerville, based on the transitional English serif typeface designed in the mid-eighteenth century by John Baskerville. It was litho-printed on Munken Premium White Paper and notch-bound by the independently owned printer TJ International in Padstow, Cornwall. The cover, with French flaps, was printed on Colorplan Pristine White paper. The paper and cover board are both acid-free and Forest Stewardship Council (FSC) certified.

Pushkin Press publishes the best writing from around the world—great stories, beautifully produced, to be read and read again.

- Gerard.
- Christel.
- Georges. Jacques.
- Allan